I0699344

ALSO BY AMY YORKE

The Wilderise Tales
The Good and the Green
The Bright and the Blue
The Ancient and the Amber
The Silent and the Silver

The SILENT and the SILVER

Book Four of the Wilderise Tales

Amy Yorke

GLASSLOOK
PRESS

For the people snuggled by the fire on a cold winter's night

WILDERISE
HEROT'S HOLLOW
Weldan House
FOSSHOLM
Gull Bay
SUDPORT
SALLIN SEA
LANDSEND
High House
NORGATE
RODAZ MOUNTAIN
LOEGRIA
ARCAS DYRNE
Castle Corycus

Pronunciation Guide & Glossary

CHARACTERS

Alison Lennox: AL-ih-son LEN-nox. A human woman of Herot's Hollow, originally Arcas Dyrne.
Keir Ainsley: KEER AINS-lee. A human man. Doctor of Herot's Hollow and Alison's partner.
Charlotte Ainsley: SHAHR-laht AINS-lee. A human woman. Sister of Keir.
Rinka: RINK-a. An orc woman. Alison's former roommate and partner of Prince Idris.
Gwenla: GWEN-la. A dwarf woman. Alison's neighbor.
Lady Sibba: LAY-dee SIB-ba. An elf woman. Schoolteacher of Herot's Hollow and partner of Weyland Gilroy.
Weyland Gilroy: WAY-lend GIL-roy. A human man. Blacksmith of Herot's Hollow and partner of Lady Sibba.
Julian Blair: JOO-lee-ehn BLAIR. A human man and childhood friend of Charlotte.

Prince Idris: PRINCE ID-riss. A dragon man. Crown prince of Loegria and Wilderise and partner of Rinka.

Princess Ceridwen (Ceri): PRINCE-ess KAIR-id-wen (KAIR-ee). A dragon woman. Princess of Loegria and Wilderise.

Leorias (Leo): lee-OR-ee-ahss (LEE-oh). An elf man. A graduate student of Winwold College and partner of Ceridwen.

Violet Lennox: VY-oh-leht LEN-nox. A human woman. Alison's mother.

Yordin: YORE-dinn. A dwarf man. Gwenla's cousin.

PLACES

Wilderise: WILL-duh-rise

Loegria: LOW-gree-uh

Arcas Dyrne: AR-cuss DERN

Landsend: LANDS-end

Sudport: SOOD-port

Herot's Hollow: HAIR-uts HOL-low

Sallin Sea: SAL-lin SEE

Caernock: KAIR-nok

Weldan House: WELL-dun HOUSE

Rodaz Mountain: ro-DAZ MOUNT-ain

Norgate: NOR-gate

Winwold College: WIN-wohld COL-ledge

Fulling: FUL-ling. The full-height races of the world: humans, elves, orcs, dwarves, mermaids, sirens.
Halfling: HALF-ling. Not a separate race; rather, the offspring of a Fulling and Quarterling or Eighthling.
Quarterling: QUART-er-ling. Races that come up to knee-height on humans: korrigans, hobgoblins, goblins, selkies.
Eighthling: EIGHTH-ling. The smallest races: fairies, pixies.

Prologue

Charlotte did not build up the nerve to approach Weldan House, her childhood home, until the third Winter Solstice after she fell over the nearby waterfall to her supposed death.

In the first weeks after she fell, she had thought of the whole thing as a bit of a joke.

Not that she hadn't been terrified when she went over. She had, of course. Not of dying—that was something that happened to old people, people who were at least thirty, not to little girls. No, she was afraid of getting hurt, of breaking her arm again and having to wear a sling for weeks. She was afraid that the trees she so loved to climb would be out of her reach, that she wouldn't be able to pay ball with the other kids in town.

She did not think of drowning, not until it happened.

Charlotte had been able to swim for years. Her
brother Keir took her down to the lake beneath the
manor and out into the water before she'd even started
school. They had learned to swim from the Lady Willana, an elf from the town on the other side of the
woods. The old lady was uniquely beautiful and graceful, and having no young children of her own, she had
taken an interest in caring for Keir and Charlotte
whenever she had the opportunity. Charlotte couldn't
picture her own mother, her having passed shortly after Charlotte was born. But when she read about
mothers in children's books and heard about them in
nursery rhymes, it was Lady Willana that she pictured.

Lady Willana had taught them well despite not having the most captive audience. Charlotte had been
more interested in splashing her brother than listening
to the elf's instructions or her stories of life in the city.
But Lady Willana had persisted, and ultimately, both
of the children learned all their basic strokes.

So when the water from the falls plunged her down
into icy darkness, Charlotte did as she had been
taught—she kicked and thrashed her arms, reaching
for the surface.

But the surface didn't come.

Charlotte's eyes stung as she pried them open under the water. The air burned in her lungs as she fought the urge to take in a breath. Lady Willana had warned her about this feeling. She said that giving into the temptation to breathe would be the death of her. That if she found herself trapped under the surface, she must do anything she could to reach the air. That she could not wait for someone to save her. She would have to save herself.

Lady Willana's advice had been well intended, but it had also been wrong.

Someone did come to save Charlotte in the end. Charlotte was drifting out of consciousness by the time the tiny korrigan pulled her from the depths and to the shore, so she never saw which of their number was her savior.

But she guessed it was Nolwynn. All of the korrigans were brave and kind, but none so much as Nolwynn. The woman barely came up to Charlotte's waist, even though she clearly had decades on the little human girl, but she had the biggest heart of anyone Charlotte had ever met.

She was infinitely patient as Charlotte struggled to come to terms with what had happened to her, not just when she fell, but what had been happening to her for the years that preceded it.

Charlotte knew her childhood wasn't ordinary. She hadn't known her mother, but she had grown up in the grandest house for miles around, so it wasn't a surprise to her to realize that the other children in the village lived very different lives from hers. But it took being given the option to live somewhere else for her to realize that her life wasn't just unordinary.

It was wrong.

By the time Charlotte had recovered from her near drowning, the search for her had begun. Keir had looked for her himself first. Charlotte hadn't seen him, but the korrigans told her when she woke that he'd been up and down the shore, above and below the falls, shouting for her. He'd waded into the water at the base of the falls and had come so close to going under the surface, the korrigans thought they were going to have to save him too.

But he'd eventually given up and gone back to the house for help. Charlotte could hear them in the forest around her, calling her name. Not "Charlotte," her true name, the name she had taken for herself. Her other name, the one she had been born with.

"Danny."

The korrigans had seen the way Charlotte had reacted to the voices searching for her. They had seen her fear, a feeling Charlotte couldn't name for herself.

And so they hid. They hid themselves and Charlotte with their magic, a magic that made them blend into the streams and the reeds and the woods. The men and women from Weldan House and Fossholm came within inches of Charlotte without ever seeing her.

And so she stayed with them as the weeks turned months turned into years. They seldom asked her questions about her life in the manor. This, Charlotte came to realize, was their way. Many others came to live with the korrigans during her time with them. Some stayed only for days, others for decades, but the korrigans rarely asked questions. The korrigans understood that there were some things in this world that didn't need to be spoken of. That there were some pains too great to share.

It took Charlotte many years to share hers. The innocence of childhood had offered her some degree of protection from it. Keir's efforts had offered her even more, although she wouldn't realize that for decades. She saw him sometimes, months after she fell. He seemed half of the boy he had been even as he grew taller. He walked the grounds and the woods silently, far too sullen for his years.

Charlotte couldn't understand then why that was. The Keir she had known had hated her. He had resented sharing with her, had taken things from her, had ruined her games and spoiled her fun. Worst of all, he had forced her to keep who she was secret.

Charlotte's fascination with dresses and dolls had been a cute little quirk of hers in the eyes of most of the household from around the time she could walk. But her father had no patience for it. He would not listen to reason about how normal it was for a child to try different things. He flew into a rage whenever he spotted Charlotte wearing a bonnet or pretending to embroider pillows as her mother had loved to do.

Keir had told her that, about their mother. He was young when she died as well, but he knew a few things about her, and Charlotte made him tell her the stories of their mother over and over again, every night before bedtime.

That was how she came to know that her mother had been certain that she was a girl when she was still in her belly, that she'd been so certain she had named her and bought her a doll. Keir told her the doll's name was Charlotte, the name their mother would have given her if she had been born a girl.

Charlotte could not explain it then, but later she would understand the feeling she had when she heard the story: she knew, deep down, that her mother had been right. She *had* been born a girl. Her true name was Charlotte.

Charlotte began to play games of pretend with imaginary friends who knew her true name. That was how Keir found out who she was. He caught her out near the river curtsying to a fairy prince, introducing herself as the Princess Charlotte of the Riverlands.

Keir hadn't been angry. But he had been afraid. He had looked all around, making sure no one had heard her, and then he had grabbed her by the shoulder. "You can't say that," he'd said. "You can't let Father hear you. Don't ever say it again."

Charlotte didn't understand then that Keir was trying to keep her safe. She had cried and shouted at him. Keir hadn't shouted back—he rarely did—but he would not budge. He didn't understand what it meant to her. They would get into the same argument again and again for years, right up until the day she went over the falls wearing a dress.

So when Charlotte saw Keir mourning her, she didn't understand it. She thought he would be happy she was gone.

On that Winter Solstice night more than three years later, it finally seemed like he was. A carriage had arrived the day before, and Charlotte had spotted them—Keir and their cousin, Rory—playing in the fields outside of Weldan House.

She had heard the shouting first. She raced to the edge of the woods, keeping herself close to the trees to let the korrigan's magic hide her as they had taught her to do. Winter had come early that year; the snows had started right after the harvest and had rarely let up since. Out in the yard, the boys were having a snowball fight.

Charlotte listened to the boys shouting and playing, their laughter echoing over the frozen ground, and felt a powerful sense of jealousy and loss.

She should be there with them.

She watched them for hours. She couldn't see them clearly from such a distance, but she could picture them. The rosy red of Keir's cheeks. Rory, breathless, crouched behind a tree, lying in wait.

If she had been there, she would have scaled the great old oak and pelted them both before they even knew what had hit them.

But she couldn't join them, not now. It had been too long. How could she explain what she had done? How could she make Keir understand why she had to leave, why she couldn't go back to the house even though she was so close?

He would be angry. And Father would be angrier. He might hurt the korrigans for helping her. They were good at hiding, but people spotted them some-times. She couldn't risk their safety for her sake.

So she reluctantly dragged herself back into the woods as the sun set. Hours later, she heard the chime of the dinner bell on the breeze. She had eaten already with the korrigans, but as delicious as their fish stew was, she longed for a taste of the traditional Solstice roast.

She would settle for just seeing it. She crept back through the woods to the spot from which she'd watched the boys earlier. There was no need to sneak— the korrigans would not be angry with her for going— but she did so nonetheless. Perhaps it was herself she was hiding from.

The windows of the manor were lit with flickering candlelight. Smoke poured from a dozen chimneys, leaving a hazy cloud over the great building.

It was so warm, so inviting. The cold barely touched her now that she had lived among the korrigans for so long, but she was still tempted by the promise of a night spent beside a roaring fire, a cup of hot cocoa in hand. It was almost enough to make her forget what had happened to her in that house.

The dining room faced the eastern courtyard where the boys had been playing. It was such a grand room that it had no fewer than eight windows. The heavy curtains had been drawn over them, but there was a gap between them on the third window from the left.

Charlotte crept over the fresh snow, passing through the bushes and climbing onto a thin ledge of stone to peer inside. The gap was narrow, but it gave Charlotte a good look at the end of the table.

Keir was there, and so was Rory. They had bathed and dressed in their finest attire. Keir was thirteen then, and this was likely his first Solstice dinner at the adult table. He was doing his best to mind his manners and look the part of the future lord of the house, but she could hear his gentle laughter at some joke he shared with Rory, could see him fighting off the fit of giggles that desperately wanted to escape.

Charlotte's breath caught in her throat as she watched. It was so…ordinary, so joyful, in a way their family dinners never had been.

She realized it then: she was right. They were better off without her.

Keir lifted a glass of amber liquid, and as he took a sip, he caught Charlotte's eyes for a moment.

Charlotte stood still as she watched the color drain from his face. He froze there, the drink still touching his lips, his eyes wide open and staring straight ahead.

As Keir lowered his glass, Charlotte bolted.

She leapt from the windowsill onto the snowy ground, not noticing the pain of the impact. Not daring to look back, to see if they were coming for her, she tore across the moonlit yard into the night.

She crossed the river—the river that had nearly killed her—effortlessly. The water was as familiar to her now as her old room in the manor, as much her home as any other place. But she didn't want to be at home. Not now.

Her feet carried her through the woods, past the korrigan's camp, up and up, to the edge of her father's land where it met the road into Herot's Hollow.

With everyone at home enjoying the Winter Solstice feast, the roads were silent and still, the only sound the quick crunch of her feet through the freshly fallen snow. Charlotte knew where she was heading.

What she didn't know was what she'd do once she got there.

Across the river, there was a line of shops with living quarters in their upper stories. Charlotte passed the tailor and the apothecary and stood in front of the third shop in the lane: Mrs. Knox's Bakery.

Charlotte looked into the window: the shop was dark, but she could just make out the empty shelves behind the counter. It looked just the same as it had the last time she had been there over three years earlier, the same simple wooden tables with the chairs stacked on top, the same hand-drawn sign, tucked in the corner:

1dz Solstice biscuits	*1s*
½ dz Mince pie	*1s5c*
Solstice log	*2s*

| *Fruit cake w/o brandy* | *2s* |
| *w/brandy* | *3s* |

The bakery was her favorite shop in Herot's Hollow, but she wasn't the only one who loved it. Next door, above a venture that had changed several times over the years (Mr. Blair's Antiques and Collectibles, Mr. Blair's Flowers, Mr. Blair's Fine Furnishings), candlelight flickered in the leftmost window of the upper story.

Julian was awake.

His family's Solstice dinner must have finished before she got there. Shadows moved at the back of the shop—Julian's father coming up with another wild scheme to make some coin, perhaps. Charlotte crept carefully along the front of the house, worried her hair (once brown, now korrigan silver) would catch the light from the streetlamps, alerting Julian's father to her presence.

Charlotte and Julian had been playing together since before Charlotte could remember. They'd run up and down the streets of Herot's Hollow, climbing the walls and the trees and generally causing mayhem.

The only thing that would get them to sit still for a minute was Mrs. Knox's chocolate biscuits. They were crumbly and rich, covered in a thin layer of dark chocolate which Mrs. Knox pressed into a swirly pattern that made you dizzy if you stared at it too long.

Not that you would have been able to. The biscuits were so delicious, especially with a big glass of cold milk from her icebox, that they seldom lasted more than a few seconds in the presence of any of the children in town. Or any of the adults, for that matter.

Charlotte hadn't had one of those biscuits in years. She wondered if Julian still stopped by the bakery on the way home from school. She wondered if he ate a biscuit (or two, or three) at one of the little wooden tables on his own now, or maybe if he'd made another friend to share them with.

Charlotte wondered if he thought of her sometimes. He must have heard what happened to her. She wondered if he believed she was dead like everyone else did, or maybe if he thought she'd run away like she often spoke of doing. Maybe he thought she'd gone to join the pirates in the Sallin Sea. Maybe he pictured her with a wooden leg and golden tooth, wielding a saber with a flourish as the stormy waters raged around her.

Or maybe he never thought of her at all.

Charlotte knelt to the ground in front of the shop. She felt around the cobblestones of the street until she found it: a perfect little pebble.

She turned it over in her hand, considering.

Should she see him again? Could she walk away, now that she was here?

No, she decided. She could not.

She launched the pebble upwards, striking Julian's window with a *tap*.

She held her breath as she waited. His shadow stirred within the room, rising from the bed and heading to the window, the silhouette of the boy growing smaller and more distinct as he approached the paned glass.

It was him. He was taller than she had expected, and his hair had been cut closer than she knew he liked it, but it was the same boy she had known.

The same boy she had grown up with. Her best friend in the world.

At least, she hoped he was. She hoped that whatever he thought of her—if he thought of her—that it didn't make him too sad.

She hated to imagine him sad.

Charlotte hesitated for a moment more. He was looking around—any moment now, he would spot her.

Then she took off and ran before he could.

Whoever he was now, he was better off without her. She was sure of it.

Chapter One

RÉPONDEZ S'IL VOUS PLAÎT

Alison

The stack of envelopes on the desk loomed before Alison.

Better get the letter-opener, she thought. That was a papercut waiting to happen if she'd ever seen one.

As she fumbled in the drawer, Willow hopped onto the desk, sending a pair of envelopes to the floor in her wake.

"You're meant to be helping," grumbled Alison.

"I'm organizing," said Willow, unperturbed. "Helping you prioritize."

The tabby cat purred slyly, her tail curling at the end. The very picture of innocence.

Alison sighed as her fingers found (gratefully, the handled end of) the letter-opener. Then she retrieved the fallen envelopes from the floor with a flick of her wrist and a thought:

Two in the hand,
Wouldn't that be grand?

"Poetry" was sort of a loose term for what Alison had come to realize was the key to controlling her magic on her own. But "silly rhyming magic" sounded much less clever and impressive than "poetry magic." No one needed to know the quality of the "poems."

Alison knew what lay in the stack of envelopes from their identical shapes: RSVPs. (A Gallic phrase, Keir had told her when they dropped the wedding invitations off at the post office two weeks earlier. Alison had never studied Gallic. "A pity, *ma chère*," Keir had replied. "It is the language *de l'amour*." His accent had been so horrendous, Alison had burst into laughter, much to his chagrin.)

"I still don't know why you bothered sending invitations to everyone in town," said Willow, pawing at the envelopes. "You see most of them every day."

"It's tradition," said Alison, someone who had little use for traditions at all.

Willow stared at her blankly, unbelieving.

"They're just so pretty," Alison admitted. "When Weyland drew such a pretty little cottage, I wanted everyone to have one."

In fact, she'd gone to a great deal of trouble to see that they had. She had taken Weyland's drawing—her little white cottage with the thatched roof, covered in winter snow—all the way to the printer in Sudport, the nearest one that could print in color. It was the very same printer that had expressed interest in printing a book of her poetry after seeing the pamphlet they had made at the summer.

But Alison hadn't brought it along. She was too busy with the wedding planning, she told herself. She could worry about the book later.

(In truth, there was a part of Alison that was frightened to see the book in print, as much as she had longed for it. It would be putting a part of herself out there for all to see, and the wedding itself was more than enough of that for now.)

"Alright," said Alison, starting in on the stack. "Let's see what we've got. Yes from Mother, oh, and she's bringing along Aunt Rose and cousin Eloise even though her invitation was only for her plus one…"

"At least she isn't bringing some man," said Willow.

Alison hadn't even considered it as a possibility; the plus one had simply been customary.

"I can't even imagine," said Alison. She didn't want to, truth be told. If Alison's mother had met anyone since her father's death, she'd never mentioned them. Alison knew that it wasn't fair to her mother to wish for her to be alone for the rest of her life, but she couldn't bear to think of someone else in her father's place. At least not at her wedding.

She sighed. A wedding was supposed to be a happy occasion, but she'd found it difficult so far not to think of who would be missing.

"Come on," said Willow. "That's three people. Surely more of them said 'yes' than that."

"Right you are," said Alison, grateful to the cat for the reminder to focus. "Ah, Ceri and Leo returned their invitations together. Both said yes."

"That answers that," said Willow. There had been a bit of a wager going on how long the princess and her Gallic *l'amour* would last, now that he was back in the same…realm? World? It was hard to say where Leo had gone exactly during their time at Winwold College, but they were grateful to have him back. And none more so than Ceri, although according to Idris, she was liable to toss him off as soon as she found some shiny new toy to play with.

Alison wasn't so sure. She didn't believe that her own experience in a strange magical world with Keir had been the only thing that pulled them together, but going through something beyond explanation certainly seemed to strengthen their bond. Perhaps Ceri's writings to Leo during his journey had done the same.

"Yes from Lady Sibba and Weyland—"

"Obviously," said Willow.

"Yes from Nigel Smalls and from Duncan Corbett, but both of them indicate they're bringing a plus one. Do they mean each other?"

"I suppose you'll have to go and ask them," said Willow. "Which is what you could have done in the first place—"

"Yes, alright, alright. But have you seen them together at the inn lately?"

"Not since you sent the invitation, although I hate going down there when it's snowing. It's so cold on my paws going over the bridge."

"I wonder…"

"Wonder later," said Willow.

Alison rolled her eyes at her relentless little taskmaster of a feline. "Oh, this one is unexpected." She paused for a bit of suspense—Willow was going to like this news in particular. "Groundskeeper Tomasar said yes."

Willow's pupils widened, her tail twitching in anticipation. "And Barney too?"

Alison smiled. "And Barney too."

Willow purred and rubbed her head against Alison's wrist. "Thank you for asking," she said.

Alison was happy to facilitate the reunion of Willow with Tomasar's sweet dog Barney, the first dog friend Willow had ever made.

"This one must be from Nolwynn," said Alison, picking up an envelope that was still a little damp, the ink of the address streaked and splotched in the corners. "The korrigans are coming. Nolwynn and another woman. It doesn't say if she's a Quarterling as well. Yes from Yordin and Marna as well, and they're bringing their three youngest."

"Seat me as far from them as possible." The cat shuddered, undoubtedly remembering the pink bow the dwarven industrialist's children had wrapped around her neck.

"Yes from Aras, Mezec, and Lydiach. Mezec has a plus one—very interesting. Yes from Brytak and Strelka, yes from Mrs. Knox, yes from Mr. Rainey. Ah, our first regrets: Dean Whittaker."

"He'd probably marry you himself if it meant never seeing the rest of us again," said Willow. "Imagine what Idris and Ceri must have done to him since we left the College."

Alison shook her head. They had made the poor man suffer enough during their time there in the autumn.

"Regrets from the office as well, but Ms. Varma enclosed a ten-gold bank note. A collection from well-wishers, she says."

That was kind, but Alison knew there weren't many in the office where she'd worked in Arcas Dyrne who would have even noticed her absence. She suspected the gift was from Ms. Varma herself.

"That's all of them," said Willow. "Nothing from Rinka and Idris?"

That was odd. Alison wasn't certain Idris would be able to take time off around Lupercalia—it was a few weeks into the spring term, after all. But surely Rinka wouldn't miss Alison's wedding.

"What's in this one?" asked Willow. She pawed at a large brown envelope that had been at the bottom of the pile.

Alison opened it. Inside was a copy of *The Loegrian Woman*, a glossy women's lifestyle magazine Alison had never once read, let alone subscribed to.

"Do you think this could be for Charlotte—" she began, then stopped once she saw the cover.

The Royal Coup—How Prince Idris Finally Fell in Love (and with a Commoner!)

And there, sitting in a grand chair with Prince Idris standing beside her, was Rinka in full color illustration.

"Is that—" started Willow.

Alison nodded wordlessly and flipped through the pages, searching for the article.

The Royal Coup
by Lady Emily Marlowe

She's elegant. She's poised. She's the envy of every girl in Loegria, Wilderise, and beyond.

You might have met her over the summer at the court events in Fossholm, a charming little hamlet in the Hill Country of Wilderise, the site of King Derkomai's latest endeavor to bring modern comforts to all of his people. You may have seen her dancing with courtiers or having tea with fine ladies. You might have even seen her steal a kiss from Prince Idris himself.

But she is not the Lady Rinka of Paistos as she once claimed.

She is simply Rinka.

On the opposite page was a picture of Rinka in Idris, this one in black and white, taken by a real picture-taker.

"I bet she loved having these portraits done if nothing else," said Alison.

"Read it to me," said Willow.

She sits across from me in Her Highness Princess Chloe's parlor sipping a cup of tea delicately, her pinkie finger neatly extended. It isn't difficult to see how people could be fooled.

"We weren't trying to fool anyone," she says, glancing back at his Royal Highness, Prince Idris of Loegria and Wilderise, for reassurance.

His Royal Highness looks dapper in the regalia of Winwold College, where he is serving as a guest lecturer for the year. He gives Rinka a nod and a tense smile. "Well, that wasn't the primary goal, anyway."

The primary goal of their charade—a charade that had everyone "quite convinced," according to Princess Chloe, was simply to see more of each other, Prince Idris explains.

Prince Idris goes on to tell a story of falling in love at first sight that, as outlandish as it sounds, I believe immediately. His affections are so plainly written on his face, I scarcely need him to speak to understand the details.

But as they are rather extraordinary, I'll include them here for your benefit, dear reader.

"This should be interesting," said Willow. "I wonder how much of the truth he told."

Alison wondered the same. There were parts of their story that made little sense without magic.

"I travel in disguise," begins Prince Idris, setting down his teacup and glancing at Rinka as if to ask her permission to share the details. Rinka nods regally. "It prevents attracting too much attention. When I ran into Rinka on the rail-wheeler, I'm afraid I looked quite down on my luck. Rinka was kind to me. She offered to mend the holes in my trousers. I was taken with her at once."

Rinka, for her part, didn't share the prince's immediate affections. "There were little things about him that didn't add up. The holes in his trousers, for one. They were in the wrong places. I thought he might have been in the picture-show."

Rinka regales me at length with her extensive knowledge of the picture-show. At one point, impressed by her erudition, I offer her a position here at The Loegrian Woman *covering the new pictures as they're released. She blushes and declines the suggestion, clearly embarrassed by her outburst. But, dear reader, if you could only see how charming she is when she talks of something she loves! (The only other subject that seems to merit such enthusiasm is the prince himself.)*

"She was on to me from the start," says Prince Idris. His eyes crinkle at the corners when he looks at her. "I'm certain she would have figured me out,

too, had it not been for a little interference from Burning Ash."

Yes, dear reader, Burning Ash. The notorious pirates hailing from the Western Isles, whose raids on innocent cargo vessels and small port towns went from a source of annoyance for the King's Navy to their top priority following their attack on an unarmed passenger ferry.

The very same ferry that Prince Idris and his new companion were traveling on.

"Of course, there was little I could do with no weapon on me. They knew my identity—knew I'd be on the boat. I foolishly attempted to challenge the pirate captain to fisticuffs, and it landed both of us overboard."

This part was definitely untrue. "A peace offering to the king," Alison explained to Willow. "He wants support for stepping up the action against Burning Ash. Idris must have dropped that in there to soften the blow of Rinka's announcement."

Miles from the shore and alone at night, Prince Idris and Rinka were all at sea. "I'm an okay swimmer," begins Rinka, but Prince Idris interrupts. "She's being modest. She's an excellent swimmer. It saved our lives." Rinka explains she learned to swim in the waters of the River Eabrun, a common pastime for those without a summer home to escape to.

"The way they talk about the common folk like they're some sort of wild species. As if most of their readers aren't common," muttered Alison, stroking her dark braid in indignation as she read on.

"We also had some help from a lovely pair of mermaids. They helped us to the shore in exchange for stories," says Rinka.

I ask them about the stories they told the mermaids, but they get uncharacteristically cagey. "Just tales of life on the land," says Rinka. She quickly changes the subject. "Once we made it to the shore, we found our way to the main road, and from there it was just the matter of a pleasant country walk to Fossholm."

But they've left out the part I wanted to hear the most—how Rinka reacted once she heard who the prince was.

"Oh, I'll admit I was a bit upset. I had grown rather fond of him, and once I knew who he was, I knew my hopes were in vain."

But once they'd arrived at their destination, Prince Idris had an idea: "Let's tell them you're a noble," he told her. "Then we can spend the summer together getting to know each other."

"It was only meant to be for the summer," says Rinka. "It wasn't meant to hurt anyone. I thought I'd go back to my life—or I'd start a new one there in Wilderise like I'd planned—and no one would need to know about Lady Rinka of Paistos."

But they found they couldn't bear to be apart. "I knew I couldn't say goodbye to her. This isn't the kind of woman you say goodbye to."

I ask if that means what I think it does.

"We'll see," says Prince Idris. He winks at me, and it's so charming I can't fault Rinka at all for wanting to keep him. "If anything happens, you'll be the first to know."

Princess Chloe steps in then to usher me out. I glance back in their direction as I leave, watch them relax as they stop holding their perfect poses. They look at peace with each other, absolutely content in a way I've seldom seen.

To pose as a courtier, to fraudulently present yourself as being above your station, is still a crime in this country, although it's one that's rarely prosecuted on its own. And yet I can't imagine the pair in that room as criminals or schemers or fraudsters or anything more than two people deeply in love, doing what they have to in a world that hasn't made things easy for them.

I hope, dear reader, that you'll join me in getting to know them before passing judgment. I think you'll be pleasantly surprised.

"Well that went as well as it possibly could have," said Willow. "No mention of magic, but the rest of it sounds like the story you told me. Did she include a note?"

Alison reached into the envelope once more.

My Dearest Alison,

Enclosed you'll find our magazine debut as well as our response to your invitation. (Of course we'll be coming! And I graciously accept your offer to be your Maid of Honor. Idris is a bit miffed he's only to be the Best Man and not being asked to officiate, but I told him to get over himself.)

We'll both be arriving in Wilderise shortly for the Solstice lighting. Then Idris will return to begin the spring term, but I'll stay behind to help you plan for the big day. I hope you haven't ordered your dress yet—I'm bringing along a stack of magazines with the latest fashions from Aunt Chloe and Ceri.

Give my love to Willow. I heard it through the grapevine that a certain canine is very excited to see her again.

All my love,
Rinka

Willow purred. "How nice of her to think of me. Is that everyone you invited?"

"Almost," said Alison. "Nothing yet from Genn and Mab, although Aras wasn't completely certain about his instruction to tuck the invitation into the hollow of a log. Maybe it never arrived."

"What about the spriggan?"

Alison shook her head. She had gone into the forest on a warmer day the week before, but he wasn't in his usual location, and she didn't want to resort to the breaking of branches method to summon him. "I'll try again the next time I head to town."

"If you can even get into town. Those 'lectric wirers are blocking half the roads. I've been stuck walking along the walls to get there."

Alison didn't point out how Willow had always preferred to walk along the wall. "It will be worth it in the end. The 'lectric lights will be wonderful for the Solstice tree lighting. Didn't you enjoy the 'lectrics at the College? The 'lectric can-opener?"

"Good point," said Willow. "Speaking of—"

Alison smiled and headed into the kitchen to feed the cat. It would be a bit more effort with the manual can opener, but Willow deserved a treat.

She had earned it after all her hard work keeping Alison on task.

Chapter Two

THE NEW MAN IN TOWN

Charlotte

"**O**w! Ow ow ow ow ow ow OW!"

Charlotte vaulted around the kitchen, hopping on one foot and fanning her open mouth wildly.

Her tongue was on fire.

Not literally, of course. But it really felt that way.

Her eyes watered as she reached for the door to the icebox. Through her tears, she could just make out the jug of milk inside.

No time for a glass. She guzzled the ice-cold milk so fast she nearly choked on it.

Ah, sweet relief. The heat was still there, but it was getting better by the second.

It was at that moment that Keir opened the door. "Charlotte? You'll never guess who I saw in Fossholm—what in name of the Gods happened here?"

For a moment, Charlotte saw the scene through her brother's eyes. She could picture herself, tears running down her cheeks, milk running from the corners of her mouth, her silver hair and fair skin dusted in cocoa powder along with half of the kitchen, clouds of flour eddying in her wake, every bowl and utensil coated in dark goo.

And all around them, the faint smell of burning.

"Oh no! The second batch!"

Charlotte reached for the oven in such a panic she forgot the oven mitt.

"The mitt!" Keir yelled just in time as smoke began to pour from the oven.

Charlotte grabbed the tray of burning brownies with one mitted hand, threw open the door with the other, and tossed the burnt brownies into the snowbank just outside.

"Ah," she sighed in relief as leaned against the door, safely inside the kitchen once more. "I didn't burn the house down."

"You didn't burn the…" Keir started, his head shaking in disbelief. "Isn't it your day off?"

"Well, yes," said Charlotte. It was funny how that look of his—those furrowed brows, the set of his strong jaw—brought her right back to childhood. Right back to wanting to lie and make up excuses to avoid his fury.

Well, not his fury. Keir had never really gotten angry with her. He often told her that he would, but he never did. She'd only realized it lately—his threats had been empty. They were only to save her from a far worse punishment that awaited her if their father found out.

But this Keir—the grown up one, the one she'd lived with for a few months since their reunion—was not unreasonable. There was nothing to fear from him.

"I wanted to surprise Mrs. Knox. I found something in one of the books you have in there on the ancient people of Anahuac." She gestured to the bookshelf in the living room. She recalled Keir's surprise when he learned that she'd developed a love of reading in her time with the korrigans; Nolwynn had been very insistent on all of the children receiving an education. "The people of Anahuac cultivated chocolate originally, and they often served it with chilies like the ones you grow in your garden. I've tried adding your chili powder to Mrs. Knox's brownie recipe, but I can't quite get the amount right. I'm close though."

Charlotte went to the hand-written recipe on the table—it was blotched with butter—and crossed out "1 tbsp" next to "chili powder." *Too much*, she scribbled in the margin. (Above it, "1/8 tsp" had been crossed out as well, with *Too little* written beside it.)

"I'll clean it all up, I promise," added Charlotte when she looked up into Keir's frowning face.

Shortly after Keir and the others had left for their trip to Loegria, Charlotte had been in town fetching tea from the market when she'd spotted a sign in the window of Mrs. Knox's bakery: *HELP WANTED.*

Charlotte had stopped by many times already since her return, and Mrs. Knox had remembered her right away. She'd served Charlotte with her favorite biscuits and listened to her stories of life with the korrigans, never once asking why she had run away. When Charlotte went in to ask about the sign, Mrs. Knox hired her as her apprentice on the spot.

Keir moved cautiously into the kitchen, trying to avoid piles of loose sugar. "Can I try one at least?"

Charlotte smiled mischievously. There was still milk left in the jug. "Go on," she said.

Keir cut a middle piece from the tray of brownies on the counter—the tray that didn't get chucked out into the snow—and took a bite.

"Mm. That's really good," he said. His brows lifted in pleasant surprise. "I can't taste the heat—oh, there it is. Oh. OH. OW."

He began to fan his tongue exactly the same way Charlotte had minutes before.

"Ow! Ow ow ow ow ow ow OWWWW!"

Charlotte pushed the jug of milk into his outstretched hand. Keir knocked it back far more neatly than Charlotte had done, but with no less enthusiasm.

"Why didn't you warn me?" Keir asked once most of the red had drained from his face.

Charlotte was doubled over laughing. "I'm sorry. I couldn't help myself. Too hot?" she asked, feigning innocence.

Keir rolled his eyes and shoved the milk jug back at her, a hint of a smile playing at the corner of his mouth. "How much pepper did you use?"

"A tablespoon."

"Are you mad?"

"Clearly," said Charlotte, then she burst into laughter again.

Her laughter was infectious. Keir tried to keep his face stern but failed quickly, dissolving into chuckles as he took a seat at the table.

"I'll put the kettle on while I clean. Tell me about Fossholm," said Charlotte, grabbing a pile of dirty dishes as she listened to her brother tell her about his day.

After all the washing up was done, Charlotte heated pot after pot of water to fill the bath.

It was a luxury she didn't really need—she could have just as easily bathed in the frigid waters of the stream outside. The adaptations she'd gained with the korrigans hadn't left her, although that might have had something to do with her weekly return to their camp in the woods outside Fossholm.

"The changes are lasting," Nolwynn had assured her. "They wear off in some of the adults after a few years away, but you grew up here. You won't change back."

Charlotte believed her, but it was more than her adaptation to living in cold water that she feared losing.

Charlotte had been born into the wrong body. It wasn't unheard of among the peoples of the world, but there just wasn't much to be done for it when it happened. The best that most people like her could hope for was dressing to match the person inside or changing their name to fit them better.

But Charlotte had been given an extraordinary gift. She had gone to live among the korrigans young, and as she grew, she found her body becoming a woman's body instead of a man's.

It wasn't painful, no more so than was ordinary when growing according to Nolwynn. And it wasn't scary, either—it felt like becoming who she had always been. The person she saw in her reflection in the lake where she'd nearly drowned slowly became the person she had always been.

The only fear she felt was that someday, she would lose it. It would be taken away from her, and she'd wake up in a body she didn't recognize, answering to a name she'd never wanted.

Still, one hot bath wouldn't hurt. It wasn't like she would find the korrigans in the stream outside Keir's house; they seldom made it up this far. And she would visit them as usual at the weekend.

And oh, the bath was so nice. It felt so good to clean all of the flour from her skin and to soak in the hot water, the fire roaring in the nearby fireplace. Keir had left to stay with Alison for the night (as he usually did), and so she had the place all to herself.

Or nearly. Dinah was there, of course, although the cream-colored cat had no interest in the bathtub. She had probably managed to find a few drops of spilled milk in the kitchen and was enjoying the treat.

Charlotte sank back into the tub, letting the warm water relax her muscles as she planned her next foray at baking—hopefully with a bit less burning, literally and figuratively.

In the morning, Charlotte arose early to head to the bakery. Mrs. Knox liked to open with the dawn, which was thankfully later at this time of year, but it meant getting there early enough to get the first breads and pastries ready before the sun rose.

Mrs. Knox was already there by the time she arrived, rolling out the first loaves. She was a human woman in her fifties, Charlotte guessed. She must have been younger than Charlotte when she'd opened the bakery, although young Charlotte had thought she was ancient on account of the white streaks of flour that never left her chestnut brown hair. That hair was more white than brown now, and Mrs. Knox was a bit rounder around the middle than Charlotte had remembered, but she was still the same kind woman that had made Charlotte feel welcome all those years ago.

On one of her first days at work, Charlotte asked her about her husband. "Oh, no husband, never has been. I just never had need of it. The name is for the business. 'Mrs.' sounds more homely, don't you think? But you can call me Moira, dear."

Charlotte never did call her "Moira," despite the permission to do so. Even as she learned more and more of the recipes and handled more and more of the business over the weeks, she still felt like a child in the shop more often than not, and it felt rude to be so informal with her elder.

"Hello, dear. I'm just getting a head start on these loaves. The Solstice rush and all. Did you want to get going with the scones?"

Scones were a quick bread, meaning they didn't need time to prove. Mrs. Knox made them on days after they were closed instead of croissants, which needed to rise in the proving cabinet overnight.

"It means we get to sleep in a little," Mrs. Knox had said with a clumsy wink when she'd explained it. Charlotte didn't mention how she regularly fell asleep at dawn during her time with the korrigans, or that waking up before it was difficult for her. She was too grateful to have something to do—something that earned her a little coin, so she didn't feel so guilty taking so much from her brother, even though he insisted he needed no payment from her.

By the time Charlotte had finished with the scones, Mrs. Knox was already on to her signature biscuits, having also started the cakes while Charlotte worked.

"You'll get faster with time," said Mrs. Knox. She never seemed to mind how long it took Charlotte. Charlotte supposed she had managed without help for all those years. Even if she was slow, she had to enable Mrs. Knox to do a bit more, at least.

"Mrs. Knox?" she asked as she emptied a jar of strawberry jam into a bowl to serve with the scones. "Why did you decide to hire someone after all that time alone?"

She'd never thought to ask before.

Mrs. Knox paused her rolling pin to answer. "I always said I was going to. I'd hire someone so I could take a trip to Gallia to try the sweets they sell in those pretty patisseries you read about in the papers, or so I could go to one of the fairy restaurants in the city, or maybe just to the beach in Sudport for a weekend. But I never did."

"Why not?"

"I don't know. The timing was never right. Too busy, not busy enough. No one looking for work, too many people looking for work that I would have felt bad for turning them away. But I'm getting older now. I'm not ready to hang up the towel yet, but I'll have to someday. And when I do, I don't want it to be forgotten, all the things I make here. They're family recipes, almost all of them, or things I read about and spent months or years perfecting. I don't want them to go just because I have. So that's why you're here."

Charlotte didn't know what to say. She'd suspected Mrs. Knox had just been lonely, or that maybe that her hands were getting tired with age.

She hadn't known Mrs. Knox was hoping to give the shop to someone someday. Maybe to her.

"I hope that isn't too much pressure," said Mrs. Knox when Charlotte didn't say anything. "It's all a long way off. You could get married and move away between now and then. But for what it's worth, I'm glad I took you on. You have a knack for it, baking."

"I've got something new I've been trying out," admitted Charlotte. She hadn't planned on telling Mrs. Knox about the brownies until the recipe was perfected, but the moment felt right. "It's not quite ready yet, but I think you'll like it once it is. You don't have to sell it or anything."

Mrs. Knox turned away from her biscuit dough to look at Charlotte. The flour dusting her cheeks didn't conceal their rosy glow of pride in her apprentice. "I'm sure I'll love it. I can't wait to try it."

⋄⋄⋄

Later that day, Charlotte opened the shop, but the usual morning rush didn't arrive.

"That's odd," said Mrs. Knox. "We were so busy all last week. It's usually our busiest time of the year, the lead up to Winter Solstice. I wonder where they all are."

Charlotte left her spot behind the counter and walked out into the street. There were people coming and going in their winter coats and scarves, parcels and packages in hand as they went from store to store and into the market square beyond, stocking up for the Solstice. A light snow had begun to fall, but that didn't seem to deter any of the crowds from anywhere but the bakery.

There was something odd, though. Charlotte could smell baking—croissants or some other very buttery pastry, to be exact—coming from across the street.

"See anything?" asked Mrs. Knox, who had come out to join her.

Charlotte pointed to the shop. It had long been empty, but now a queue had formed outside the door.

"It looks like they've finished moving in, then. I saw a carriage unloading last week, but they had gone before I could greet them. Can you read the sign from here?"

"Cheese Shop, it says," said Charlotte. The sign hanging above the door was new and hastily painted. "There's something else in small letters."

She crossed the street to get a better look.

"And Baked Goods," called back Charlotte, her heart sinking.

Who would move in and open a bakery right across the street from Mrs. Knox's?

Charlotte moved towards the door. Nigel Smalls, the bard she often ran into at the inn, was waiting in the queue.

"Bad luck about the shop, but I've heard the cheese croissants are to die for. I had to come and try them for myself. Nothing against Mrs. Knox, of course, but it is nice to have something new now and again," he said, clapping Charlotte on the shoulder cordially.

Charlotte shook off Nigel's hand and peered into the window.

There behind the counter, handing out cheese croissant after cheese croissant, was someone she thought she'd never see again.

Julian.

Chapter Three

GIFTS AND SURPRISES

Rinka

The journey to Wilderise aboard HMS *Delphine*, the flagship of King Derkomai's navy, was a far-cry from the ferry Rinka and Idris had taken over the summer.

The *Delphine* was less a battleship and more a floating parade, a grand, opulent display of the wealth and power of Loegria and of the king's might and influence. She was equipped with luxurious quarters for traveling courtiers and diplomats, her dining hall catered elegant meals with fresh ingredients from its latest port of call, and there was even a live band that played after dinner concluded.

Rinka enjoyed her time aboard so much that she regretted that the journey itself was so much quicker—the *Delphine* moved at twice the speed of the ferry.

But Rinka and Idris had not chosen to ride with the *Delphine* for its luxury or its speed. The *Delphine* was equipped with something very important for Rinka's present mission: a *DIALS* system; DI(stance) A(nd) L(ocation) at S(ea).

The only thing that might help Rinka find the mermaids that saved their lives.

The *DIALS* system was intended to spot enemy vessels, particularly the underwater vessels the dwarves on the continent preferred. But since Loegria was still technically at peace—Idris explained that that was becoming more of a technicality as tensions rose in the continent, although so far, Loegria had managed to keep out of it—the *DIALS* system had gone unused for some time. It turned out the Admiral in charge was only too happy to put *DIALS* into use once more, and he made no comment about the frivolity of the mission.

"Got your sea legs under you yet, my lady?" asked Idris when he joined Rinka on the deck. It was freezing cold outside, but Rinka had found it stuffy in the bridge with the naval officers.

"Not 'my lady' anymore. Just Rinka," she replied with a smile wide enough to show her fangs.

"You'll always be my lady," said Idris. He wrapped his arm around her shoulder, rubbing her upper arm for warmth.

Rinka pulled back to look at him. "That's the corniest thing you've ever said. Are you ill?"

Idris laughed. "And here I was trying to be romantic. What did she say about me in the article? 'My affections are plain?'"

"'Plainly written on your face,' I believe. Obvious. Not plain as in boring."

"Ah, that's it. So I'm meant to be more mysterious and withholding." Idris withdrew his arm and backed a pace away.

He was such a smart arse. He was lucky he was so handsome there in his suit and bowler, the cold sea air bringing color to his cheeks.

Rinka could not resist him.

"The time for mystery has passed," she said. She closed the distance between them again and lowered her voice to a whisper. "I've seen bits of you you've never seen yourself."

Idris's almond eyes flared. The time for mystery had ended, perhaps, but she still managed to surprise him every once in a while. "There's more I could show you—"

Admiral Northwood cleared his throat behind them. Rinka and Idris sprung apart. "Forgive me, your royal highness. Miss Rinka. We believe we've spotted something out in the reef."

Rinka looked to the Wilderisen coastline. They had passed the southeastern corner and were heading up the coast towards Gull Bay, just where they'd spotted the mermaids the first time. "Is there any reply?"

Admiral Northwood, a greying human who had begun to gap the buttons on his naval uniform, smiled apologetically. "I'm not certain the mermaids have the ability to signal back. Some of my crew claim to have spotted them in these waters, and we're picking up something large and stationary not far beneath the surface. Too large for an underwater ship."

"A city?" asked Rinka.

"Could be," said Admiral Northwood. "We haven't spent much time here. We're too slow to take on Burning Ash."

"This is slow?" asked Rinka. She hadn't answered Idris's sea legs question, but truthfully, she was struggling a bit. As beautiful as the *Delphine* was, her speed was rough on the stomach.

"And too obvious. Burning Ash can spot us from miles away. We're setting course for the reef now. We should arrive shortly if you want to accompany me on the dinghy."

"Of course," said Idris. "And the trunk?"

"Already loaded, your highness."

Rinka gave Idris a look as they followed the Admiral: *the dinghy?* She looked out over the water. It was so cold up here there were chunks of ice floating in the sea. She was grateful they'd gone overboard in the summer—going in the water now would be death.

Idris sighed as he noticed her look. Then he took off his jacket and helped her put it on. "It's a good thing I have dragon's blood."

Rinka didn't argue with that. The warmth of his skin was a blessing at this time of year.

Admiral Northwood helped Rinka into the dinghy as Idris checked the trunk. It was a large wooden thing with a great iron clasp and a set of iron weights to carry it under the surface.

"I'm sorry to your crew that they'll have to lower us with this thing. It must weigh a ton," said Idris.

But he needn't have apologized. The dinghy was lowered with a great 'lectric pulley. They hit the cold water with a splash that thankfully landed outside of the small vessel.

"Now let's see if we can find some mermaids," said Admiral Northwood as a Halfling crew woman started rowing.

"Do you know how to signal to them?" asked Rinka.

"I was going to ask you," said Admiral Northwood.

"The rowing will bring 'em if they're out here, Admiral," said the crew woman. "That's if they didn't hear the *Delphine* coming."

The waves were calm as she rowed, but the vessel didn't have the ability to cut through them as Idris's water boat had. The bobbing up and down was more than Rinka's stomach could take. "How long do you think we'll be—"

Before she could finish the question, she heard a laugh.

It wasn't the giggly laughter of Cordy and Em. It was a deep laugh, warm and musical.

"Did you hear that?" asked Admiral Northwood. "It sounded like it came from the sea."

"It's them," said Idris. "It has to be."

Admiral Northwood pointed the crew woman in the direction of the laughter.

"What if we can't find the girls?" Rinka asked Idris. It hasn't occurred to her that they might find different mermaids.

"I'm sure they can help us find them."

"You think they all know each other?"

"That's not what I—"

There was more laughter then. A dozen or more different laughs and the sound of bodies breaking the surface.

"We're surrounded!" shouted the crew woman.

Admiral Northwood instinctively reached for his sidearm. "Who's there?" he called. "Show yourselves!"

A head popped up over the side of the dinghy. It was a bald man with very dark skin and the characteristically large round eyes of the mermaids. "Testy, aren't they? For landfolks who showed up in our waters?"

A second head popped up on the other side. This one was a man with red hair that was like Rinka's, only much more vibrant even when wet. "Typical landfolks. Bringing all their metal and their trash into our ocean."

"What are you doing here, landfolks?" asked the bald man. "What business do you have with the king of the ocean?"

"The king of the ocean?" muttered Admiral Northwood. "I am Admiral Northwood of King Derkomai's Royal Navy. We have business with two of your kind. With whom am I speaking?"

The red-headed man laughed. "He just told you. That's the king of the ocean, mate. Are you thick?"

"King Olo, at your service," said the bald man, pulling himself up onto the dinghy to bow, his fish tail flopping over the stern.

"King Olo, we're trying to find the young mermaids Cordy and Em. Er, Cordelia and Maisie. We have a gift for them," said Rinka, jumping in to hopefully avoid an international incident over the sovereignty of the ocean-dwelling peoples.

"Ah, Nora's girls," said the red-headed man. "What did they do this time?"

"We didn't do anything!" shouted a familiar voice from behind a floating block of ice.

"Not us!" came another familiar voice.

"Oh, that's too bad. I suppose you won't want your gift then. As king of the ocean, I'll just take that—"

"WAIT!" shouted one of the girls. They both came splashing over with incredible speed.

"Oh, it's you again," said Cordy as she propped herself up on her elbows to look inside the dinghy, her wet blonde hair matted across her face. "Em, look. It's the orc and the weird guy."

"How dare you! This is the crown prince of Loegria, Prince Idris—" began the crew woman.

"The prince?" squeaked Em excitedly. "You didn't tell us you were a prince. He can do magic too, King Olo!"

Rinka shot a nervous look at Idris, but he simply shrugged his shoulders. While they had concealed his use of magic in their magazine interview in order to avoid further antagonizing the king, it wasn't as though the royal family's magic was a secret. "I did what I had to in order to survive."

"Of course, your highness," said the Admiral.

"We heard there was a present," said Cordy.

Rinka smiled at the girls. "We wanted to thank you for saving us. We didn't know what to get you, so we brought you a few things from the land we thought you might like."

Rinka opened the chest to show the girls what was inside: a mirror, a hair comb, a doll with red hair, and a spying glass.

The girls leaned over and reached for the items, picking each up and asking about its use before discarding Rinka's explanations in favor of their own.

"It's for poking fish when they won't stop bothering you," Cordy told Em regarding the comb as she poked her in the arm with it.

"Ow!" said Em.

"We appreciate your gift to our girls," said King Olo, willfully ignoring the chaos to his right. "Is that all you came for, landfolks?"

"King Olo," said Idris in a serious tone that Rinka had seldom heard from him. "We owe a debt to your people. Is there a way we can repay it?"

King Olo nodded gratefully. "We've seen fewer shipwrecks and burning vessels lately," said King Olo. "But still, there is much of your garbage in our waters. If you are the prince as they say you are, maybe you can put a stop to it."

"I'll see what I can do," said Idris, nodding back.

"Goodbye, girls!" Rinka called after Cordy and Em, who were already swimming away with their gifts, weighted trunk forgotten. "And thank you!"

"We'll take the trunk as well," said the red-headed man. Idris helped Admiral Northwood chuck it over the side.

"Next time you come, bring a diving bell," said King Olo. "I'll give you the grand tour."

⁕

Gull Bay was unrecognizable when Rinka and Idris made it to the shore a short time later.

"Mostly military," said Idris, gesturing to the people coming and going along the docks and to the *Delphine* out at anchor. "The Burning Ash cleanup operation."

When they'd arrived in the summer, the town had seemed abandoned. But Burning Ash was known to make use of small towns—often to the point of their abandonment, like Gull Bay—in between voyages.

"They staged an ambush a few weeks ago. Three ships captured. The others won't be returning here anytime soon."

"I suppose it's for the best," said Rinka.

"You have pity for the pirates?"

"If they were ordered to attack by the king or his court and then betrayed, it seems pretty unfair. But I suppose they got what was coming to them."

Idris laughed entirely too loudly as he led her from the docks to the waiting carriage. "Of course, my dear, they'll have plenty of soup for us in Fossholm…"

Rinka was bewildered. "Soup?"

"Yes, soup, your favorite," said Idris. He waited until a group of men in naval uniform had passed. "Careful what you say with these men around. You never know who might be listening."

"Of course. I'm sorry," said Rinka. She had gotten used to their habit of openly criticizing the king. But they had agreed to play a part, to make nice with the king in order to gain Idris's seat back at the table. It was Rinka's idea, and it had taken some convincing to get Idris onboard. It wouldn't do at all to ruin their plans before they'd even truly begun.

"I'm not sorry you said it," muttered Idris. "Only sorry you need to be sorry."

"Something you could change one day," said Rinka. "To give people the power to speak their minds, even if it's critical."

"Just as long as I don't have to listen to all the idiotic things they have to say," said Idris.

Rinka punched him in the shoulder.

"Ow!" said Idris, rubbing his arm.

Rinka felt a little bad because she was trying to be playful, but that probably really hurt. "Sorry," she said, kissing the spot where she hit him, and then she quickly added: "But don't be so condescending. At least half of the things *you* say are idiotic."

"Idiotic and sexy?" Idris looked at her with his bedroom eyes. They were alone in the carriage; Idris's guards were outside and in a separate carriage behind them.

"Just idiotic. Although…"

Idris pulled her legs into his lap. "Although?"

Rinka whispered in his ear, "Alright, clever clogs. Tell me the most idiotic and sexy thing you can think of."

Idris responded immediately. "I'm so hot for you, I'd burn your mouth like a bowl of soup."

"Extremely idiotic. Mildly sexy. Two points out of five, good effort, but you'll have to do better than that."

⚜

The carriage stopped not too long after, which surprised Rinka. "Are we there already? I thought it was fifteen miles to Fossholm."

"There's something I wanted to show you first. Come on."

Idris led Rinka from the carriage into a green field in the shadow of a mountain. The last of the sun's rays were shining on it, melting off a thin layer of snow. "It's a nice enough field, I guess, but I was actually looking forward to that soup. It's been a while since lunch…"

Idris sighed. He led her by the hand to a pile of rocks on the ground. A shovel had been wedged between them. He pulled the shovel from the pile and handed it to her. "Go on," he said.

"Go on and what?"

"Break ground," said Idris. He smiled slyly.

"These are the ruins of the king's estate?" The "ruins" weren't much to look at. Now that Idris had shown her the corner, she could sort of see how the rock wall must extend in either direction, although the stones themselves were so covered in grass or moss that it was difficult to tell where the walls ended. "I thought they'd be a bit more…substantial."

"To tell the truth, I did too, but it's for the better, really. We'll build it all from scratch."

"Right here?"

"Right here. Come on. This was more or less your idea. Break the ground."

Rinka hesitated. To open a university in Wilderise had been something they'd come up with together. Idris wasn't in a hurry to go back to his post at the

King's College once his year at Winwold was over, and Rinka wasn't in a hurry to go back to the city at all. But Rinka wanted to make an impact on the world—her time amongst the royals and at Winwold had led her to believe that the common folk deserved more than they had, and that education was the key to making that happen.

And what better place to do it than Wilderise? It would be the first university here since the burning of the colleges in the Great Wars. It was the target of the king's modernization plans.

And it happened to be near where their friends lived.

"The king approved?" asked Rinka, her hand gripping the shovel.

"Well," said Idris. He ran his hand through his dark hair. "There was a compromise. A manufactory will be built as well."

It was inevitable, Rinka supposed. The king had set his sights on a manufactory in Wilderise long ago. "But Idris, the dangers—"

"I know what they're like. It doesn't have to be that way. Father has given me wide latitude to set the standards for workers. I'll be limiting working days, preventing children from working, and hiring people in charge of safety."

"The king agreed to all of that?"

Idris smirked. "He thinks I'll fail. He's wrong, of course. Oh, and over there—" Idris pointed in the direction of Fossholm. "That will be the hospital. I'm going to ask Keir to help manage it."

Rinka looked at Idris, awed. "Is it really going to happen? A college, a manufactory, a hospital? All right here?"

"All right here. All thanks to you," said Idris.

Rinka looked down at the ground. "I didn't do anything—"

Idris placed his arm on hers. "I wouldn't have done it without you. I couldn't have. You were right about me. You told me when we met that I had the power to change things, and you were right. It's going to take a long time, and I'm sure we won't get it all right the first time, but maybe we can do things better here."

"Why, Idris. That sounded almost optimistic." Rinka pushed him playfully on the shoulder and then leaned over and kissed him on the cheek. "Thank you," she said in a rare moment of sincerity.

"Of course. Now, are you going to break the bloody ground before I freeze to death?"

Rinka laughed and took his hand, placing it on her hand holding the shovel. Together, they dug up a small patch of dirt near the ruined wall.

"One down, five million more to go."

Chapter Four

THE OTHER BAKER

Charlotte

Charlotte wasn't sure how she'd recognized Julian straight away. It must have been twenty years since that Winter Solstice night when she'd seen him last. When she'd run from him before he could see her.

He was taller now, even taller than he'd appeared in the window that night. Broader, too, though still on the lean side for his height. His skin was the same warm brown Charlotte remembered, and he still wore his black hair closely cropped to his head, but he'd grown a light beard now as well.

It suited him.

"He looks familiar," said Mrs. Knox as she joined Charlotte across the street. "Not one of our regulars, but maybe I served him at the Midsummer Festival?"

"No," said Charlotte. "He lived in town once. A long time ago. I wasn't around when his family left, but he may have been just a child then."

Mrs. Knox grabbed Charlotte by the arm. "It isn't. Tell me that isn't Julian Blair."

"I think it is," said Charlotte, tucking a strand of her silver hair behind her ear.

"Oh, well, that changes everything! You and Julian spent so much time together at the shop. It must have made an impression on him too. This is all a misunderstanding. Let's go clear things up with him."

Mrs. Knox tugged Charlotte forward, but she didn't move.

"Come on," said Mrs. Knox. "Unless you think it isn't a good idea."

"No," said Charlotte, backing away. "I'm sure he didn't mean anything by opening the shop. But I have to go. I have to—"

Charlotte ran back into Mrs. Knox's bakery, straight through the shop, past a sole customer waiting at the counter, and into the backroom, where she slammed the door behind her.

❧⊙⊙⊙☙

Charlotte's pulse pounded in her ears. Her chest was tight; she couldn't seem to get a good breath.

What was Julian doing here? Charlotte knew he had left Herot's Hollow a long time ago. It had taken her years to work up the nerve to come back into town—at night, of course, while everyone was sleeping—but when she did, there were strangers living in his family's house, and a charity shop had moved in downstairs.

Why had he come back here? And why had he opened up a bakery of all things?

"Well, that was a waste of time," said Mrs. Knox when she returned. "Managed to sell three loaves of bread to Mr. Rainey there, though. He's got a full house at the inn. What're you doing on the floor?"

Charlotte had lowered herself to the ground near one of the cupboards. "Just catching my breath."

"Are you alright, girl? You look a bit peaky." Mrs. Knox rested the back of her hand on Charlotte's forehead.

Charlotte gently pushed it away and got back on her feet. She could go through the crisis of what to do about seeing Julian again after work. "I'm fine. Did he not remember you?"

"Oh, he remembered me, alright. Said he didn't mean to do me any harm, but he needs the 'baked goods' to bring people into the shop. It's the cheese he's really wanting to sell, and the wine. The croissants are just meant to get folks in the door. I asked him if that meant he'd give them up once folk in the town know he's there, and he said, 'We'll see.'"

The cheer had slowly drained from Mrs. Knox's voice as she spoke. A scowl set into the lines of her face. For the first time since she'd started working there, Charlotte could see Mrs. Knox's age.

"It's not like I've never had competition before. But just across the street, and at the busiest time of the year. And just as I've taken on my first employee…"

Her eyes flashed at Charlotte, and Charlotte realized what she meant: if the bakery didn't recover, there was a chance Mrs. Knox would have to let her go.

"I'm sure it will be fine. We make far more than croissants here. Once the novelty wears off, they'll be back. You'll see."

Charlotte made a decision then that she hoped she wouldn't regret. "I'll go and speak to him."

Mrs. Knox tried (unsuccessfully) to hide her delight. "Oh! Well, if you could. I'm sure it couldn't hurt. You two were as thick as thieves from what I remember."

Charlotte nodded slowly, dazed.

Mrs. Knox grabbed her hand and gave it a squeeze. "It'll be alright, girl. He'll be glad to see you. Don't worry."

Charlotte shot Mrs. Knox a grateful look. Then she pulled herself up and pushed herself out of the bakery before she could change her mind

⋯

The line had gone by the time she made it to the cheese shop. She stood at the door, her hand on its brass handle, and looked through the glass.

Julian leaned against the wall behind the counter. He look tired but satisfied, a small smile on his lips, his eyes gently closing.

They snapped open at the sight of Charlotte.

Julian stood up straight, brushing his hands on his apron, and he gestured at Charlotte to come in.

Charlotte felt her pulse pound in her throat. Did he recognize her?

She willed her hand to turn the knob. *For Mrs. Knox,* she thought. *For the bakery. For my job.*

"Hello, Miss," said Julian. His voice was warm and rich and deep, far deeper than Charlotte had been expecting. "I'm almost out of the croissants, but I've saved one here just for you."

He winked one of his big brown eyes. It wrinkled the skin at its corner pleasantly. *Just for you*, he'd said.

He must have remembered her.

Charlotte's legs felt as though they were made of lead as she dragged them to the counter. She became suddenly aware of herself—the flour on her apron, the silver hair coming loose from its bun, her hands rough from kneading dough and frequent washing. She should have gone home and straightened up before coming here. This isn't how she wanted him to see her for the first time. For the first time since…

"I promise I don't bite," said Julian with a chuckle. "Try the croissant. Go on."

Julian reached beneath the counter and pulled out a gorgeous croissant in a piece of brown paper. The pastry was a lovely golden color, flaky and perfectly rolled. Charlotte knew the work that went into laminating the dough, knew the trick of keeping the butter cold to stop the layers from going flat. She'd made croissants at least four times a week since she'd started at Mrs. Knox's three months earlier, but she had never made a croissant that looked this good, not even on her best day.

"It's not poison," said Julian as Charlotte hesitated. "I made it fresh this morning. There's a Gallic cheese inside. It's quite strong, a little gamey, but it goes nicely with the butteriness of the pastry. You aren't allergic, are you?"

"No, I…" said Charlotte, then she took a bite when she could think of nothing else to say.

Oh, dear. It wasn't just good. It was *heaven*.

Charlotte watched the smile spread across Julian's lips as he watched her eat. "Not bad, is it?"

Not bad? "It's insane. The salt, the butter—is that a bit of pepper in there too?"

"Just a pinch. They were meant to have ham, but my delivery has been delayed. I thought they need something to give that savory bite."

"It really works," said Charlotte with her mouth full.

Julian laughed. "I can see that."

Charlotte was already eating the last bite. She didn't mean to eat it so quickly, but it was just too damn good to stop. She looked back at him, embarrassed.

"I'm glad you liked it," he said. "You know, I thought I knew just about every pretty young lady in town. Are you new around here?"

Charlotte froze.

He didn't recognize her then. And did he say *pretty*?

"I'm guessing you're a baker as well. Mrs. Knox's daughter? Or niece, perhaps? The silver hair is unusual. Fairy ancestry?"

Charlotte swallowed the last of the croissant. She needed to say something. But what? She scrambled for a lie. Maybe she'd go with what he'd said: a niece of Mrs. Knox. The fairy ancestry wasn't too far from the truth; the korrigans and the fairies were closely related.

But it wouldn't do. He was here now, and by the looks of the shop, he wasn't going anywhere anytime soon. If she lied, he'd just find out the truth from someone else in town.

No, she was just going to have to be brave and tell him the truth. If she could face Keir, if she could admit to him what she'd done after everything she put him through, she could do the same for Julian. Her best friend in the whole world. "I'm not new in town, not exactly. I lived here long ago, the same as you."

Julian cocked his head to one side. "You know who I am then. It seems I'm at a disadvantage." He looked her up and down, trying to place her. "I don't remember any silver-haired girls in town, and I'm fairly certain I wouldn't have forgotten you."

Charlotte felt the heat of his gaze. Was he flirting with her? She laughed in spite of her nerves. If he knew who she was… "I look a bit different now, and I go by a different name. My name is Charlotte, but you once called me Danny."

"Danny?" Julian repeated, confused. And then: the dawning look of recognition. *That's the one*, thought Charlotte.

The smile vanished from Julian's face. He stumbled backwards, his hand grasping for something to hold onto but finding only air. "No. It can't be. Danny died. Everyone said Danny was dead."

Charlotte took a deep breath. Of course he had thought she was dead. They all had.

Julian was hunched over against the wall behind the counter. He looked utterly broken. Here he had stood just minutes earlier looking perfectly content, and now this. This is what she had done to him.

She couldn't do this. The guilt overwhelmed her. She had let her best friend in the whole world think she was dead. He was just a child, too. How must it have felt for him when she didn't come back?

How could she have been so selfish?

"Is it really you?" Julian's voice was tiny. It was the voice of eight-year-old Julian. Of the boy that still lived inside of this man's body.

There was no going back. There was no taking away that little boy's pain. But maybe she could give the gift of closure to the man. It wasn't enough, but it was all she had to give. "Julian, it's me."

Julian's eyes lifted to meet hers on the mention of his name. For the briefest moment, she could see the glisten of a tear before he blinked it away. "You're alive."

"I'm alive."

"And you're…" Julian gestured to Charlotte's body.

"I'm Charlotte," she said.

"Well, Charlotte," said Julian. "Tell me everything."

Charlotte told Julian everything that had happened to her. He had already known what things were like for her at home, so it wasn't that much of a surprise to him to learn that she'd chosen to let everyone believe she was dead rather than return there.

"But you could have told me," he said. He had sat her down at a table in the front of the shop. When a customer came, he helped them, but not before begging her to stay until they left. "I wouldn't have told anyone. You know that, right?"

Charlotte had thought about it many times. "I knew you wouldn't tell, not intentionally, anyway. But someone might have seen us together. I couldn't risk being seen. It would have given me away."

"But you could have sent the korrigans to get me. Or you could have come yourself after you changed. I doubt anyone would have recognized you then. I didn't."

Charlotte smirked. "I could tell you didn't recognize me."

Julian's eyes widened. "I'm sorry if I was a bit…forward. You're just…" He looked down at his hands as if they were very interesting, as if he wasn't humiliated at all. Not in the slightest. He cleared his throat.

Charlotte's ears were hot. He was attracted to her, that was plain to see. And she would've had to have been blind not to see how handsome he'd become. Gods, that beard…but they were *friends.* Long lost friends, reunited at last, and that meant more than any fleeting attraction could.

"You were always wearing those dresses, even back then. I knew it was a joke, but I also knew it wasn't. I'm surprised to see you again, but I'm not surprised you're a woman. If that makes sense."

"But you're surprised that I'm a pretty woman," said Charlotte. She wasn't sure why she was repeating it. She was teasing him, she decided. As friends do. "Don't worry; that surprised me as well."

"Yes, well, you already know what I think. You let me make that clear. A couple of times."

"Sorry," said Charlotte, grinning. "I couldn't resist."

"Charlotte?" Julian grabbed her hand from across the table, and the years were gone. He was Julian, holding her hand to help her up the tree on Orchard Lane. Julian, running with her in the fields by Weldan House chasing rabbits. Julian, the sun on his brown skin, his laughter on the summer breeze.

"I'm so glad to have you back."

⚬⚭⚬

"Well?" asked Mrs. Knox when Charlotte returned. "What did he say?"

The bakery. Charlotte hadn't even mentioned the bakery. "Oh Gods, I forgot—"

"It's alright, girl," said Mrs. Knox, pulling her into a hug. "Are you alright?"

Was she alright?

"I'm great. I'm…wonderful."

"Oh, I'm happy to hear it. I told you. Everything's going to be okay."

Charlotte pulled back from the hug. She took Mrs. Knox's hand. "I'll go back there tomorrow and talk to him about the bakery. I'm sure he'll listen."

Tomorrow, then. After twenty years apart, twenty lost and lonely years, she'd see him again.

Tomorrow.

Chapter Five

A SMALL GIFT

Alison

Rinka and Idris were late to arrive at Weldan House, but Alison didn't mind. It gave her some much-needed time with Keir, which had been in short supply since their return from Winwold: there was a flu going around.

"Mr. Parsons is recovering well," Keir said as he arrived around midday. He dropped his medicine bag to the ground and collapsed into a wingback chair across from Alison by the fire, exhausted. "I was concerned about his cough, but it doesn't seem to be progressing to pneumonia."

Alison brushed a strand of his dark hair behind his ear—it was getting long. She kissed him on the forehead. "That's good to hear."

"Did Ms. Murray give you your gift?"

"I haven't seen Ms. Murray today." The maid was likely busy preparing for Rinka to arrive. Although Rinka wouldn't be mistaken for a noble on this visit, they would still give her the courtesy of a lady's maid as an honored guest of Prince Idris.

"Come, it's in the kitchens." Keir took Alison by the hand and led her through the long corridors of Weldan House, down the stairs, and into the enormous kitchens in the basement.

"Is that a 'lectric stove?" asked Alison, walking over to a shining dwarven steel range that was at least twice the size of her little oven back in Arcas Dyrne.

"This is the first room in the house to have the 'lectrics finished."

Alison marveled at the new mixers and toasters and two 'lectric frigerators: no expense had been spared. Not that she expected any less from Lord Ainsley, who thankfully was spending the Solstice at court with the king and would not be arriving back in Wilderise until the 'lectrics were all finished in the spring.

"Over here," Keir called from across the room. There on a counter sat a small package wrapped in brown paper with a little red bow tying it together. Behind it sat a mirror.

"It isn't Solstice yet," said Alison. "I haven't even gotten your present."

"This isn't your Solstice present. It's for the wedding." Keir smiled, kissing Alison's hand and placing it on the ribbon.

Alison pulled on the red ribbon and opened the paper. Inside was a box: *'Lectric Curlers for the Discerning Young Lady.* "Oh!" said Alison. It was a curling iron just like the one she'd used in Winwold. She'd never owned one herself, even when she'd lived with 'lectrics in Arcas Dyrne. "Aren't they quite expensive?"

Alison hadn't become accustomed to having such nice things without needing to worry about the cost. But the first of their cut of the solar generator profits had recently arrived. It was only a month's worth, and all the costs of production had been taken out, but it was still more than Alison had made at her number-crunching job. A lot more. And Keir had received a share too, and that was on top of his allowance from Weldan House and his earnings as a doctor, though Alison knew he severely undercharged for those services.

"Do you not like it?" asked Keir. "I didn't know which one to get. I sent a letter to Ceri, and she recommended this one from a catalog she receives. She sent along a copy of it—"

"No, it's perfect." Alison kissed him on the cheek. "Can we try it out?"

"Of course," said Keir, opening the box and plugging the iron into the wall. "That's what the mirror is here for."

Alison and Keir waited as the curling iron heated up. It was very exciting to see something buzz to life with 'lectricity here in Wilderise. "The sun powered that. Isn't that strange to think of?"

"It's incredible," said Keir. "And without the town being underwater." He hovered his hand above the iron. "It feels pretty hot."

Alison let her brown hair down from its typical braid and carefully picked up the iron by its wooden handle. "Ceri did this for me at Winwold. I think you pinch this little lever and hook it over the hair like so," she said, grabbing a small section near the front. "And then you twist and hold it for a short while."

Alison looked at Keir watching her in the mirror. He was equally parts fascinated and terrified, likely due to the proximity of such heat to the flesh of her ear. "Careful…" he warned as she pulled the iron a bit too close.

"Ow!"

"Are you alright?"

Alison quickly released the hair from the iron to take a look at the spot where she'd gotten her ear. "It's okay. Just a tiny spot."

"Let me see."

Keir moved the curl out of the way—it was quite a pretty little coil, and it was holding well—and examined her ear. "Not a bad burn. I have an ointment in my bag that will help it heal. I'm not sure this is something to use on your own, though," he said, holding up the iron. "Shall I give it a try?"

"Only if I can give you a curl or two as well," said Alison, loosening the strand of hair she had tucked behind his ear earlier.

Keir smiled. "Deal."

⁕

By the time Rinka and Idris arrived, Keir and Alison vaguely resembled a pair of poodles.

"Good Gods, man. Did the 'lectrics turn you feral?" asked Idris as he climbed from the carriage.

"Is that from a curler?" asked Rinka. "Can I see it?"

Alison brought Rinka to see the 'lectric curler while Keir invited Idris for a pre-dinner drink in the parlor. "Are you ready for the wedding?" asked Rinka. Alison helped her remove her cloak and traveling hat so they could curl her hair as they caught up. "I'm happy to help arrange things once this Solstice festival is done."

"There's still a lot to do before the big day," Alison admitted. "The first dress appointment is the day after tomorrow—will you be able to make it?"

"I wouldn't miss it."

"How's the Solstice planning going?"

"From Gwenla's last pigeon, it's a bit of a mess. I'm meeting her in Herot's Hollow tomorrow. Something to do with the tree—I don't suppose you'd like to get involved?"

Alison laughed. "Gwenla made me promise to stay out of it and focus on the wedding, but I'm happy to help."

"Good because I think we need all the help we can get."

After Alison and Rinka had finished with the curls and gotten dressed for dinner, they rejoined the men.

"You've gone feral as well I see," said Idris, putting his arm around Rinka and tugging on a red curl. "It suits you."

Keir cleared his throat—the pair of them were really too much sometimes.

"Right then," said Idris. "Tell me again why you won't let me officiate your wedding."

Chapter Six

THE BAKER'S APPRENTICE

Charlotte

Charlotte stayed late at the bakery, taking her time with the dough they'd use to bake the croissants in the morning.

She wanted them to be absolute perfection. Julian had managed to avoid letting the cheese and the butter escape from his perfect little pastries, and she knew she could do the same if she was slow and careful about it, returning the dough to the icebox frequently to avoid letting the butter melt.

They wouldn't be filled with cheese, of course. The cheeses they used when baking were soft, young cheeses that went into sweet frostings, and they were supplied by the young orc Brytak when he made deliveries from the family farm. If things had been different, perhaps they would have turned to Julian to supply them.

Maybe there was still a chance of it, if Charlotte could talk him around.

As she walked back to Keir's house after closing up the bakery, she glanced at Julian's shop. She could go talk to him tonight. There were a few customers inside, but he'd likely close up shop soon. Maybe she could ask him if he wanted to get a drink at the inn.

But then what would she say? "Hey Julian, nice to see you again. By the way, why did you move back to town and open a competing shop directly across the street from one of the only people that was nice to us when we were little hellions? Are you an arsehole now?"

No, she'd need to workshop it a bit more. Hopefully Mrs. Knox could manage one more day before Charlotte brought him to his senses.

Back at Keir's house, Charlotte bathed off the flour and sweat in the frigid waters of the nearby stream. She thought about swimming down to see Nolwynn for advice; the korrigan wasn't the most diplomatic creature, but she had managed to leave the king's castle with her head intact, so she must have had some talent for negotiating.

But Charlotte was too tired to make the journey. All that kneading and rolling still wore her out. She had no idea how Mrs. Knox had managed it alone all those years, or how Julian could manage it now.

Not that his arms looked weak. In fact, they'd look plenty strong enough. He had a lot of muscle straining against his rolled-up sleeves…

Was it bad to think of him this way? It certainly was unexpected. Charlotte never thought she'd see Julian again. She had no idea where he had gone or any way to contact him. She wasn't sure she would have even if she had known how, for his sake. But when she had seen him last, they were children. And now? Would it be so bad if things changed between them? They were different people now. Would it be terrible to explore whatever spark they seemed to share?

Charlotte decided that it wouldn't be terrible at all. But she also wasn't going to be making the first move. She'd get him to cross out the "And Baked Goods" somehow, and then, if he proposed spending time together, she wouldn't say no.

It was sorted. The plan was flawless.

The plan failed.

Everything had been going so well. Charlotte had come in to Mrs. Knox's early to check the croissants. They looked nearly perfect: the almond-filled batch had risen just a tiny bit less than the plain and choco-late-filled, but if she put them at the end of the counter, no one would notice the difference.

They baked beautifully. She could see a couple of drops of chocolate coming out of a few of them, but they were still her best effort yet. The pastry was light and impossibly flaky and perfectly golden brown.

Mrs. Knox had been so impressed with them, she'd nearly cried. "That's the way to save us," she'd said. "If we can't join him, we'll beat him."

That hadn't been Charlotte's intention; she still thought she could get Julian to stop competing with them. But she had been inspired to try her best to show that she could bake as well as he could. Nothing com-petitive about it. She just wanted to see if she could rise to the challenge, and she had.

The line outside of Julian's door wasn't quite as long today, and some of the usual customers had made their way back into Mrs. Knox's shop. Perhaps he'd stopped selling the croissants without Charlotte need-ing to ask.

Still, it would be nice to see him again. After the morning rush had gone, Charlotte headed across the street. There was no one in Julian's shop when she en-tered. No one except Julian, who paced anxiously behind the counter.

"Everything alright?" asked Charlotte. It didn't seem he'd heard the doorbell chime.

"Mm?" he asked without looking up. Then he spotted her. It stopped him in his tracks. "Charlotte. You're back."

"I am," said Charlotte. "There was something else I wanted to talk about."

"Please, sit," said Julian. Whatever had been bothering him earlier seemed to vanish from his thoughts in Charlotte's presence. "What did you need?"

You can do this, she told herself. He seemed like a reasonable man. Never mind that he said no to Mrs. Knox. Maybe she offended him somehow. By…being aggressively nice. That must have been it…

"Charlotte?"

"Sorry." He was looking at her quite intently from across the table. He looked exhausted—there were large bags under his eyes where there hadn't been any yesterday. "Julian, I wanted to ask you. Why the baked goods?"

"Oh, that," he said, relaxing back into his chair. "It's simple, really. Cheese and wine smell wonderful, but the aroma doesn't carry far. You can smell the baking out in the street. It brings in foot traffic. It's important for business."

That was what he'd told Mrs. Knox. "But Julian, there's already a bakery on this street. I know you knew that because you once lived next door. We spent so many days in Mrs. Knox's shop."

"Of course," said Julian. "I remember it well. I'm still very fond of it."

He didn't seem to see the connection in what Charlotte was saying. Could he have not realized his business could hurt Mrs. Knox's?

"But what is Mrs. Knox to do if you take all her customers?"

Julian smiled and shook his head. "Oh, that seems unlikely. I don't primarily sell baked goods, not yet at least."

"Not yet?"

"The cured meats were supposed to arrive this morning, but they still aren't here. I've made all of this bread, but I've nothing to serve it with, and not many of the croissant customers were willing to take a loaf. I guess they prefer the familiar. Maybe if I cut some into samples and give them out in the street—"

"Julian, I don't think you're understanding me. You made bread? You're trying to sell sandwiches? That's half of Mrs. Knox's business. More than half."

Julian shrugged his shoulders. "Then the market must be good for it here. I don't know what you want me to say. It isn't personal. I loved that old woman—although I guess, she couldn't have been that old, considering she's still alive. But I have a business to run. And this is the way it works."

Charlotte didn't understand. Julian was acting as if he didn't have a choice about what kind of business to run—maybe that was true. Maybe his father had come by the cheese business somehow, and he was just following the plan. But even if that were the case, he didn't have to bring his business here, to this very street. To a street that already had a bakery.

"Why here? Why did you come back here?"

Julian's face fell. "Are you not happy that I'm here?"

"Of course I am," said Charlotte. "But I don't understand. This isn't the city. This town can't support two bakeries; there just aren't enough people. If you keep taking Mrs. Knox's customers, she'll have to close."

"Ah," said Julian. "I see. And then you'll lose your job. But in that case, I'd be doing well enough to take you on. You don't need to worry." He rested his hand on Charlotte's.

She snatched it away. "I'm not worried about me. I'm worried about Mrs. Knox. I don't know how you could be so cruel to her. What happened to you?"

Julian pushed his chair back from the table and stood abruptly. "I learned a lot of hard lessons, including that you can't let your feelings stand in the way if you want to survive. Mrs. Knox has been baking the same things the same way for decades. If she wants to win, she'd better come up with something new. Because I've got a lot of tricks up my sleeve, and I don't plan on holding back."

Charlotte's mind reeled. Hard lessons? What had Julian gone through that had left him so cold?

"Julian—"

"Charlotte, if you'll excuse me, I believe that's the meat delivery at last." He ran out the door in the direction of the approaching carriage, leaving Charlotte alone at the table.

What had just happened?

Mrs. Knox looked hopeful as Charlotte returned, but her face quickly fell when she saw Charlotte's.

"No good?" asked Mrs. Knox.

Charlotte shook her head. "He's changed. I don't know what happened, but he wouldn't listen to reason."

"Did he feed you the same story about needing to lure people in with the smell?"

"Just the same."

"Well, two can play at that game." Mrs. Knox led Charlotte into a little office she kept in the back. "See this?" She pointed to a line on an order form. It was for the merchant in Sudport that supplied the chocolate, almonds, and other goods they didn't grown in Wilderise.

"Coffee: 2s per pound, whole bean. Oh, of course."

There weren't many coffee drinkers in Wilderise, but Charlotte had met one once before: a dwarf who stayed with the korrigans for a year or so when she was still a girl. He'd ground the beans every morning by hand, then he'd made the coffee over the fire in a metal pot with a basket in it. The smell was so strong he'd attracted several of the townsfolk, forcing Charlotte to hide in case one of them recognized her.

One day, after the townsfolk had gone home, he'd let her try a taste. It had been a terrible letdown. The smell was so good, but the taste was so awful and bitter.

"You'll like it when you're older," he had told her, but she hadn't believed him.

"Do you think it will work? It smells good enough to get people inside, that's for sure, but the taste…"

"Did I hear you say coffee?" Lady Sibba stood in the doorway to the office. She must have entered the shop as they were walking to the office.

"Yes," said Mrs. Knox, clearly a bit uncomfortable about Lady Sibba's intrusion but unwilling to miss an opportunity. "After Ms. Waters left and closed the café, there hasn't been anyone selling it in town. I thought I might change that."

"Thank the Gods! I went down to the café every morning before school. I've been dying since we got back from the college and couldn't find any in town. It's quite addictive, you know."

Mrs. Knox raised her eyebrows at Charlotte. "Even better."

"Now, would one of you be able to help me with a custom order? It's for Weyland's Solstice present. I want to do those cinnamon biscuits that he loves so much, but I wonder if you could make them a bit bigger. Maybe spell out his name. Is that too cheesy?"

"Of course," said Charlotte, and she led Lady Sibba back to the front to place her order.

After Lady Sibba had gone, Mrs. Knox came back with the order form. "What do you think? If it doesn't sell well brewed, there are a few recipes that call for it. I have a book somewhere from the continent…"

Charlotte wasn't sure. On the one hand, the coffee was likely to draw in customers just as Mrs. Knox hoped. But on the other hand, it would mean giving up on cooperating with Julian and entering into a culinary arms race against him.

But what choice had he given them? They'd both tried reasoning with him. Maybe if they beat him at his own game, he'd have no choice but to give up the bakery side of things. He'd still have the cheese, the wine, and the meat to sell. Maybe he'd even buy some of their bread to sell with it.

"Do it," said Charlotte. "I'll go up to Weldan House when I see the korrigans this weekend and look for recipes with coffee, too."

"Wonderful!" said Mrs. Knox. "And if any of the things you've been working on are ready for a taste test, let me know. It's time to up our game."

⌘

Charlotte left the shop open at the end of the day. There were two more customers coming in: Keir and Alison had an appointment to plan their wedding cake.

Mrs. Knox had Charlotte help her with the sample cakes. They made them with the smallest cake pans, and Mrs. Knox showed Charlotte how to pipe on the icing into intricate swirls and shells and rosettes.

The finished mini cakes were absolutely adorable. It was clear to Charlotte where Mrs. Knox's work ended and hers began, but Mrs. Knox assured her she'd get better with practice.

Alison and Keir arrived just after sunset. Charlotte let them in and led them to the table where they'd set the cakes.

"They're all so wonderful!" said Alison. She walked around the table, admiring them from all angles. "And so many choices. It's a good thing we haven't had dinner yet."

"We've just come from the new shop across the street," said Keir. "Have you seen him yet, Charlotte? It's Julian Blair."

Charlotte and Mrs. Knox shot each other a meaningful look. "Yes, we know," said Charlotte.

"Then you know he's selling croissants in the mornings?" asked Alison.

"I'm afraid we do," said Mrs. Knox. "We did try speaking with him, but it appears he doesn't intend to stop."

"Not even for an old friend?" asked Keir, looking at Charlotte.

Charlotte shrugged. "He remembered me, but it didn't seem to matter." Not regarding the bakery, at least. "He seemed more worried about his business than anything else."

"I suppose that makes sense," said Keir. "His father having gone to debtors' prison and all."

"How do you mean?" asked Charlotte. Julian had mentioned "hard lessons." Was that what he had meant?

"His family left in a hurry around the time I left for university. I saw the father's name in the papers some years later: imprisoned for unpaid debts."

"Maybe Julian helped him pay them off," said Charlotte.

"Or maybe he's still doing so," said Alison.

"Let's let our customers enjoy what they came here for," said Mrs. Knox. She gestured for Keir and Alison to sit down. "We can talk about what it means for our plans later."

Charlotte watched as Alison and Keir tried each cake in turn. First, they tried the traditional choices: vanilla with Gallic meringue buttercream between the layers and white fondant on top for the bride, and a simple fruitcake soaked in brandy for the groom.

"It's nice, but I want something a bit…more, I think," said Alison.

"I think we'll all be sick of fruitcake after Solstice," said Keir.

Next, Mrs. Knox pointed them to one of the trendiest options. "This is the same vanilla sponge, but the filling is a sweet cream with raspberry jam, and I've done the outside in a white chocolate ganache with sugar flowers. Or rather, Charlotte has done it."

"You made this, Charlotte?" asked Alison.

"I helped," said Charlotte, blushing. "Mrs. Knox did most of the work."

"That's not true. Charlotte did half of these herself."

"Well done," said Alison. "They look—and taste— incredible."

Charlotte appreciated the compliment, although she was fairly certain Alison would have said the same even if Charlotte had done a terrible job.

The real test of her skills would be Keir's reaction. He wouldn't insult her in front of her boss, but he also wouldn't lie if he wasn't impressed.

"It's good, but it needs a little something else," he said after trying a chocolate sponge with chocolate ganache for the groom's cake. "Why not add a bit of the pepper? A bit. Not too much."

Charlotte grinned. "Not as much as the other night?"

Keir told Alison and Mrs. Knox about Charlotte's experiment and little prank.

"Is that the recipe you've been telling me about?" asked Mrs. Knox. "Let's try adding the pepper to the ganache. Unless you were only joking."

"No, not at all," said Keir. "She did go a bit overboard with the brownies, but the first bite before the pain began was delicious."

"Just what every baker dreams to hear. 'It was delicious until the pain started,'" said Charlotte.

They tried the rest of the mini cakes: a tropical-inspired cake with mango and coconut that Alison adored but not quite as much as the raspberry, a carrot cake that even actual medical doctor Keir thought was too healthy for a wedding, a lemon poppyseed cake that Keir said felt too much like breakfast at university, and a white chocolate sponge with champagne and strawberry buttercream that left Alison quite torn.

"They're both so lovely," she murmured, mouth half full, her fork going back and forth between the raspberry and the strawberry champagne cake. "Keir, I need help."

Keir tried both cakes in turn, but he too was undecided.

"What if we did them both together?" suggested Charlotte. "The vanilla sponge with the champagne Gallic meringue buttercream, then we'll add in both strawberry and raspberry jams, and we can top it off with the white chocolate ganache."

"And those lovely little sugar flowers," said Alison. "What do you think?" she asked Keir.

"If you're happy, I'm happy," he said.

"Then that's exactly what we'll do," said Mrs. Knox. "Three tiers for the bride, one for the groom?"

Alison was confused. "Why should the bride's cake be bigger? Can we do them both with two tiers?"

"Of course."

As they were leaving, Keir pulled Charlotte aside. "You did a wonderful job. If you hadn't told us you helped, I would have thought Mrs. Knox made them all. They looked professional. Well done."

Charlotte beamed with pride. She just may have found her calling here in Mrs. Knox's bakery.

If they could only keep it in business.

Chapter Seven

THE SOLSTICE TREE

Alison

In the morning, Alison ran into Gwenla out in the lane on the way to her planning meeting with Rinka.

"Finnli, put that down!" cried Gwenla. Finnli was holding something small and furry.

"I found it sleeping in the wall," said Finnli. The dwarf boy, a son of Gwenla's industrialist cousin, was generally quiet and well-behaved, but he had an insatiable curiosity that often got him into trouble. "Look. It's blonde like me."

Alison came over to see what he was holding. "It's a little dormouse," she said. "They sleep all winter, you know. Better put it back now so it can get its rest."

"Do as she says, boy," said Gwenla, sighing.

Finnli walked back along the wall, singing a song to the dormouse as he went.

"He's a sweet thing really, Gwenla."

"I know," said Gwenla. "I can't fault the lad. He's been quite a help with the decorations. Fearless on a ladder. I've never seen a dwarf like him."

"I've seen one," said Alison, looking at her neighbor, who was elderly in age but not in temperament. "How's the Solstice planning going? Rinka said you might be in need of help."

"Oh, I told her not to trouble you. You have enough on your plate with the wedding, I'm sure."

That was country villager talk for, "I really do need your help, but I know asking would be an imposition, so I'd like it if you offered." Alison knew it well by now.

"The wedding planning is mostly just ordering things and waiting on them to be ready. I've got plenty of time to help. Tell me what you need."

It turned out there had been a mix-up with the Solstice tree delivery. There was a farmer up in the mountains near Fossholm who grew most of the Solstice trees for Wilderise. The fir trees that grew nearby would have worked well enough, but the farmer grew them specially for the purpose, taking extraordinary care to grow the trees to be perfectly tidy and full of branches for hanging ornaments. Orders were placed months in advance. But the tree that had been delivered to Herot's Hollow for the first 'lectric Solstice lighting was the wrong size.

"Thirty feet, we ordered. If that tree's even ten feet tall, I'll eat my hat."

"So you want me to help you get a team together to go into the woods and find the perfect tree," said Alison. "There are a number of firs on the Ainsley property that would do." It would just take most of the strong people in the town to haul it back, if thirty feet was what Gwenla wanted.

"I actually had a simpler idea. Would you mind asking the spriggan to help us? If you think it wouldn't offend him, of course."

"I'm sure the spriggan would be pleased to be asked either way," said Alison. And she had been meaning to make her way back into the woods to invite him to the wedding. "When do you need it by?"

"Well, three days ago, ideally," said Gwenla. "I was going to ask Weyland today if he'd mind leading the charge into the woods if you didn't have time."

"I'll go today. I've got to go 'round Weyland's tomorrow—I can ask him then if I don't find the spriggan today."

"Perfect," said Gwenla, pulling Alison into a hug. "Thank you. You're a great help as always."

Alison hoped Rinka wouldn't mind her missing the meeting; it seemed her task was critical to the Solstice preparations, after all. She went back to the cottage to put on a heavier cloak before heading to the forest—it looked like snow.

The forest was perfectly silent as the snow began to fall. It was so peaceful and still that Alison had to stop for a moment to breathe it in. She closed her eyes, listening to the silence. It was hard to imagine this was the same forest that burst with life and energy in the spring, the song of dozens of birds filling the air, the trickle of the stream over the rocks like chimes in the distance. Today, there was nothing but the snow. When Alison opened her eyes, a lone ray of sunshine cut through the clouds and shone through the bare branches of the trees, lighting up the ice that coated them like diamonds. Alison blew out a breath, watching the little cloud that formed fade into the freezing air around her. She touched the snowflakes on her dark braid, felt them melt to water on her fingertips before tucking her fingers back into the warm mittens Gwenla had knitted her.

It was so beautiful. She truly felt lucky at that moment, to live in a time and place where such beauty could exist. She felt grateful to have played a part in saving it. As much as she loved 'lectrics—and she truly did love them—she couldn't imagine they were worth the cost of such a place vanishing from the world. The world was meant to be wild and free and beautiful. And if they had to take from it, they would only take what could be replaced.

Alison found the spriggan near the grove where they'd first met. He was sitting in the snow, the branches of his arms and legs collecting a fine layer of white powder.

"Hello, again," he said when he saw her approach. "You've come alone this time. Do you require my help once more?"

"Yes," said Alison. "Although I also come bearing an invitation."

"Tell me what you require first."

Alison explained to him the need for a tree to decorate for the Solstice. "It's a tradition. Not a very old one in this part of the world, but people love to see them covered in ornaments and lit up with lights. This year, the lights will be 'lectric for the first time."

"How peculiar. A tree wearing jewelry. Like the ring you wear?"

Alison held out her left hand to show the spriggan the sapphire ring that had once been cursed. "Can you feel any magic on it?"

"I feel nothing more than your own magic. My, how it's grown since you were last here. Were the fairies helpful?"

"A bit," said Alison with a laugh. "We also nearly died there, but it all turned out alright."

"That's good," said the spriggan without concern. He, too, had nearly killed Keir on their first meeting. Perhaps there was a connection between practitioners of magic and a disregard for mortality—Alison made a note to keep an eye on it. "I can help you with this tree. There's an old fir on the hillside you will like."

"Thank you," said Alison. And then, thinking of what she'd felt standing in the woods alone, she added, "May I plant a seed to replace it in spring?"

"That's very kind of you. Yes, you may. I will help you find a good spot to make it grow. And now, what of your invitation?"

"Have you ever heard of a wedding?" asked Alison.

"No," said the spriggan. "What is this 'wedding'?"

"It's where two people that love each other make each other promises and exchange rings."

"But you already have a ring."

Alison smiled. "This is an engagement ring. It symbolizes an intent to marry."

"So much jewelry. So many rocks. I can see why you like the ornaments on the tree. Very well. Why do you tell me of this 'wedding'?"

"It's customary to invite people who mean something to you to a wedding. I'd like you to come to my wedding to Keir."

"But I am not a person. Do I mean something to you nonetheless?"

Alison laid her hand on the spriggan's shoulder, grateful he was in his smaller form today. "You do. You've helped us quite a lot. We're grateful."

"And Keir? He would like me to be at this wedding even though I tried to kill him?"

"He would." Alison knew Keir wasn't quite as fond of the spriggan as she was, but he had come back here after the first time. He knew the spriggan no longer posed a threat.

"Very well, Alison Lennox. I will come to this wedding."

Alison Lennox. She hadn't heard her full name in a long time. After the wedding, she supposed she would be Alison Ainsley.

She would have to give up her name. Her father's name. It was all she had left of him.

"Have I said something wrong? You are upset," said the spriggan.

"No, no," said Alison, although she could hear the tears in her voice. "I'm sorry. It's nothing you said. Just something I hadn't thought of yet. There are lots of feelings around weddings."

"As long as I have not caused you offense. I will let you go now, Alison Lennox. I will bring the tree at sunset so that you may cover it in jewelry. I would like to see if once it's wearing its jewelry."

"Of course," said Alison. "Come see the lighting in—" Alison counted on her fingers, "—four nights."

"In four nights," said the spriggan.

⚜

Back in town in the afternoon, Alison caught up with Gwenla and Rinka at Weyland's forge.

"Oh, you're back already," said Gwenla, her hands full loading a cart with shiny silver ornaments as big as her head. "Did you find the spriggan?"

"The tree should be arriving shortly," said Alison.

"Excellent news. Finnli, did you get the star?"

The little dwarf boy slowly came over holding a brass-coated star that was half as big as he was. "It's heavy," he said, tilting a bit as he walked.

Rinka rushed over just before he toppled. "Maybe you can help with the tinsel." Rinka gestured to a box filled with light strands of silver foil on string.

"Okay!" said Finnli.

"Do you think it'll be enough?" asked Strelka, Weyland's orc apprentice. "Do you know how big the tree will be?"

Alison realized she hadn't specified that with the spriggan. "I'm not sure. I forgot to tell him. He seemed somewhat confused by the entire ritual…"

"Well, we'll just have to make do with what we get," said Gwenla.

"It doesn't take long to make the ornaments. If you think we'll need more…"

Just then, there was a loud crash from up on the mountain.

"What was that?" asked Rinka.

"Avalanche?" asked Gwenla.

"Not enough snow for it," said Strelka.

And then the footsteps began. *THUD. THUD. THUD. THUD…*

"What's going on?" asked Weyland. The enormous human man entered the forge from his shop bearing another box of oversized ornaments, his pale brow drenched with sweat.

"I think that's our tree," said Alison. The thudding footsteps continued, growing closer by the minute.

Everyone put down whatever they were carrying and went out to see.

"Up there!" said Finnli. He pointed off the road up the mountain to where the trees were shaking, dropping the snow on their branches to the ground in an unmistakable path.

"Oh my Gods. It's enormous," said Gwenla once the tree finally came into view.

It spoke to the awe of everyone involved that they let the statement pass without comment.

"It has to be at least thirty feet," said Alison.

"At least," said Strelka. "Maybe forty."

The spriggan itself was nearly as tall as the tree now. He carried the Solstice tree over his shoulder like it was nothing. The tree itself was an incredible fir with hundreds of delicately thin branches that would be just perfect for the ornaments and 'lectric lights.

"This way!" said Gwenla as the spriggan made it to the forge. She marched out in front of him without fear, leading the spriggan into the market square where the vendors had just cleared their stalls for the week. The others trailed behind, with Weyland dragging the cart full of ornaments.

The spriggan lowered the giant fir into the tree stand. Strelka, Rinka, and Weyland tightened the bolts, while Alison and Gwenla filled buckets of water from the pump.

"Are these the ornaments?" asked the spriggan. He leaned over the cart, lifting a silver ball which looked small in his enormous wooden hands.

"Would you like to help us decorate?" asked Alison.

Gwenla nodded enthusiastically. "We'd appreciate it very much."

"I would like to give the tree its jewelry. Where does this one go?"

"Anywhere!" said Finnli. "We're going to cover it up so it shines when the lights are on."

"The lights should go on first," said Weyland, gesturing to the boxes that had been delivered earlier in the week.

"These lights do not shine," said the spriggan.

Alison nodded. "Not yet. They will soon, once they finish connecting the 'lectrics. Lightning will flow through these cords, and then the light will shine."

"A tree glowing with lightning. How strange people are."

The spriggan lifted the end of the cord of lights from the box that contained them. There were hundreds of light bulbs hanging from the cord of the size that Alison used in her lamps back in Arcas Dyrne.

"They'll see this tree from Sudport," said Rinka.

Following Gwenla's shouted directions, the spriggan wrapped the lights around the tree. The tree was a bit bigger than the original plan, so they had to use a string of lights intended for the market square to reach the bottom.

"I think we're going to need more ornaments," said Strelka. "I'll get started on them."

"Alison, would you join us back at the forge? I had a question for you," asked Weyland.

"Sure," said Alison, happy to leave the others to the decorating. She enjoyed the outcome of decorating a Solstice tree far more than the process itself.

Weyland led Alison inside the shop and to a counter where he kept the finer goods. He pulled out a small velvet tray and handed it to Alison.

"Here are some of the options," he said, continuing a conversation that had been cut short a few days earlier by Keir's arrival. "There's the typical gold, of course. Dwarven steel is strong."

"Too strong," said Alison, picking up a ring inlaid with a knotted design. "Keir says they're difficult to cut off in an emergency."

She'd been fishing for information to inform the wedding band Weyland had agreed to make for weeks.

"There are jeweled options too," said Weyland, holding up a ring set with a large diamond. "You could match your sapphire."

Alison couldn't picture Keir wearing jewels. "He's too practical for that."

"Maybe a signet ring? The Ainsley family crest? I imagine he won't receive one from his father."

Signet rings were popular with some of the nobility, but Alison didn't think Keir would want to flaunt his family name in such a way. "I don't think so."

She picked up the rings one by one until at last she spotted a silver band with a delicate filigree. "What about this? Could you make it a bit simpler? Remove the leaves, make it in gold?"

"Hmm," said Weyland, examining the ring. "Simple design. Soft. Just enough detail to be interesting. Sounds like Keir."

Alison laughed—she knew Weyland meant the ring, but it wasn't a terrible description of Keir himself.

"Now I could use your opinion on something," said Weyland as he brought out another tray.

This tray held rings sized for smaller hands. "For me? But I just want a simple gold band to match my engagement ring." She had already told Weyland this.

"No, for Lady Sibba," said Weyland.

Alison couldn't believe it. "Do you mean—"

"Shh," said Weyland. "I'm not sure yet. I don't know if it's something she'd even want."

"But you want to marry her!" Alison whispered, struggling to contain her excitement. "Weyland, congratulations!"

"I originally thought Solstice could be the moment. But Sibba hates the cold so much, I don't know. I want it to be special. *If* I go through with it."

"What did you get her for Solstice?"

Weyland rubbed his red beard anxiously. "Nothing as of yet."

Alison rolled her eyes at him. "It's next week. If you aren't going to give her the ring, you better think of something." Honestly, men were hopeless.

Well, some of them. Alison suspected the cupboard in Keir's house that he tended to stand in front of whenever she visited might be hiding something. She had stuffed her own cupboard full of gifts (including a couple made by Weyland himself) several weeks prior.

Weyland, on the other hand, wasn't quite as much of a forward thinker. He was a good man though, really, and he meant well. Alison would just have to help him a bit in the romance department.

"She does wear a lot of jewelry," said Alison. "If not a ring, what about a necklace?"

"I was thinking—never mind, it's a silly idea."

"What? Come on. I won't tell anyone. What is it?"

Weyland came out from behind the counter and led Alison to a desk in the back. In a drawer, he pulled out a brochure. *See the Rock: An Unforgettable Island Holiday.* "I got it in Sudport on the way back. There's a ship that leaves from there."

"It's perfect! She's been talking about going for ages. You could meet her family. That would be a lovely place to propose," said Alison, pointing to an illustration of a sheltered cove surrounded by palm trees. "And even if you didn't, think of the art you could make while you were there."

"I wanted to talk to you about that too," said Weyland, putting the brochure away for now. "I've decided to sell Strelka the forge. There's enough coin coming in from the generators to keep me going without it."

Alison gave Weyland a quick hug—or as much of a hug as she could manage considering her tiny arms could barely wrap around him. "That's wonderful. What will you do with all the free time? Please tell me you're planning to draw more."

"I am," said Weyland. "I wanted to see if you wanted to work on the book again. To finish adapting the pamphlet we made, or maybe to start on another project. I like to paint the scenes on their own, but I like it better with words."

Alison had debated this privately for some time. The coin from the solar generators gave her the freedom to pursue her poetry if she wished to, which is all she'd wanted since she gave up her number-crunching career.

But there was part of her that was afraid. "What if people don't like it? Or what if they do like it, but I don't like it? What if selling my poetry turns it into a chore I hate?" The poetry writing had begun as a ploy to make more coin, but it had become a part of how she saw the world. It had become a part of her magic.

What if putting it down on paper for others to see ruined it?

"The way I see it, you have something to say, and people ought to hear it. The world is a better place when people share the beauty they see in it." Weyland patted Alison on the shoulder. "They're good poems. It would be a shame to keep them to yourself."

"Thank you," said Alison. "I'll think about it."

That night, when she returned home, she retrieved the manuscript she and Weyland had taken apart to fit into the pamphlet.

There had been some kind of order to it, but now the pages were stuffed together, some of them torn, others upside down.

She read a few lines of one of the poems:

In the meadow,
The clouds walk on fluffy legs,
While overhead,
A swan swims through clear blue skies.

Maybe there was something to what Weyland had said. She couldn't help but see the flaws in what she had written, but she could see the beauty in it too.

Maybe beauty was meant to be shared.

She slowly began to reorder the pages and to insert new ones, scribbling down new ideas as she went.

Chapter Eight

THE COMPETITION BEGINS

Charlotte

When Alison and Keir had left the bakery, Mrs. Knox congratulated Charlotte on a job well done.

And then they returned to the matter of Julian. "Debtors' prison? Do you suppose that's why Julian came back here?" asked Charlotte as they cleaned up the plates and prepared the dough for the next morning's croissants.

"I don't see why he would. Surely he could have made more coin in the city. Or anywhere in Loegria, really. Why come back to a small town that already has a bakery?"

"There's really only one way to find out," said Charlotte.

The next day, after the morning regulars had come (or at least the few of them who remained loyal to Mrs. Knox), Charlotte headed back across the street to see Julian again.

The queue was back in front of his store.

"Solstice biscuits," said Mr. Smalls. Charlotte joined the queue behind the bard. "Ginger snaps and shortbread. I've heard they're to die for."

Solstice biscuits? Those didn't even have cheese in them. "The nerve on him," she said.

"Mrs. Knox makes fine biscuits, of course," said Mr. Smalls. "But look." He pointed to a customer leaving the store. In their hands was a pretty blue tin with white snowflakes on it. "He gives them to you in that tin. It makes for a nice Solstice gift, don't you think?"

Charlotte begrudgingly admitted that it was a good idea. Mrs. Knox sold her biscuits in the more traditional paper box tied up with ribbon. "He does seem to know what the people want."

Charlotte waited her turn, and then she gave up her place in the queue when a few more people arrived so that she could speak to Julian privately.

When at last his customers had gone, she asked him if he had time to chat.

"It looks like things have died down for now," said Julian, "but I hope you'll forgive me if we're interrupted."

Charlotte was certain that Julian would not miss a single customer, come the hells or high water.

He looked better today. She imagined the Solstice biscuits had been easier on him than making the cheese croissants alone. And he must have been relieved with the meat delivery finally arriving, although she imagined that meant he'd also be taking away their lunch crowd today.

She didn't know how to broach the topic she'd come to discuss. But she wanted to understand if Julian was in some kind of trouble. If he was, perhaps they could help him.

She decided there was no delicate way to say it: she'd just have to tell him what she knew. "My brother Keir mentioned some kind of trouble with your father. Is that why you've come back here? Is that why you're hellsbent on taking the bakery's customers?"

Julian laughed. "This again. No, it has nothing to do with my father, although I will say that particular experience did teach me a lot. I spent most of my adulthood working to pay off that man's debts only for him to turn around and remarry the moment he was released. He left me with nothing. No, that's not true. He left me with a lesson: the only one you can rely on is yourself. I've told you I'm not out to hurt Mrs. Knox. I'm not trying to take the bakery's customers. I'm trying to grow my business. That's all."

Charlotte had felt the way he did once. In her painful childhood years, she had felt she had no one to rely on. But Nolwynn had taught her to trust others again. She had been lucky to meet someone who could show her that there were people in the world who were kind and trustworthy, people you could rely on when you needed help.

It seemed Julian hadn't been so lucky. "I'm sorry to hear that." She wanted to say something to him about being able to trust her, of how she remembered their friendship and wanted to help him, but she didn't think he'd believe her. "Can I ask why the cheese and wine?" It was clear to Charlotte that his true passion was baking. Or if not his passion, then his talent.

"High profit margin items. The only real investment is time. There was a shop very much like this one across from the prison. I took a job there with a hard old human and learned everything he knew. When it became clear my father would never repay the sacrifices I made for him, I started crafting my own cheeses at home. I'd take cultures Mr. Harrow discarded, bottles of wine he said would never sell. He told me to throw them out, but I took them home instead, building my stock to set out for myself."

"But you didn't steal anything from him? Anything he would've wanted to keep?" The thought had come to her, and she'd said it before she could stop herself.

If Julian had been desperate and convinced he was alone in the world, what would have kept him from theft?

Julian shook his head, backing away from her. "Honestly, Charlotte, is that how little you think of me?"

"I didn't think you would," said Charlotte, embarrassed. "I'm just trying to understand what you went through."

"Well, it wasn't a good time, I'll tell you that much, but I'm no criminal. I learned what I needed from the man, I took what he discarded, and I built my own business from the ground up. It seemed a fair exchange for my labor, which he grossly underpaid me for. The market will decide if my venture is worthwhile."

But there was something else that had been bothering her. A question he'd left unanswered the last time they spoke. "Why did you choose to open the shop here?"

"I couldn't afford a shop in Arcas Dyrne. The rent there is too expensive. I needed to go somewhere smaller to start out."

"Is that the only reason?"

Half of a wistful smile flashed on Julian's face before it returned to neutrality. "I was happy here once. This was the last place I was happy."

A sentimental answer, and the only one that didn't seem connected to coin. Perhaps there was some of the old Julian left in there after all.

"I know you feel as if I'm your enemy, but I'm not," said Julian. His eyes were soft and warm as he looked at Charlotte. It stirred something within her. "I do want us to be friends again. I'm glad you keep coming back here. Now that you see why I've done it, does it change anything?"

She could see that Julian was sincere. He truly wanted to reconcile.

But he hadn't conceded at all, and from the sounds of it, he didn't intend to. "I'm afraid I can't stand by and let you take down Mrs. Knox's business. If you believe so much in the free market, perhaps we should let it operate as intended. Good luck to you, Julian. May the better shop win."

⁂

"We'll need something to keep us going until the coffee gets here," Charlotte told Mrs. Knox when she returned to the shop. She filled her in on what Julian had told her and how she didn't think they would be able to win him over with kindness. "Maybe if we beat the pants off of him at his own game, he'll give in and cooperate."

"I don't love it," said Mrs. Knox. "It doesn't feel like it's in the Solstice spirit. But what choice do we have? Even if we make it through Solstice, we can't lose our Lupercalia chocolate sales. Your brother's wedding will tide us over for a bit—he refused to accept my discount, by the way. Such a generous lad."

That gave Charlotte an idea. "Keir could invest in the shop. I'm certain he'd want to see it succeed."

"No, no. I won't have him invest in a failing shop. No, you were right. We're just going to have to win. I've got my recipe books in the back. When it's slow, let's go through them and try out anything we think could be a hit."

They spent the day in between customers—and there was a lot of time in between customers, unfortunately—trying out biscuits. The good thing about biscuits is they were quick to bake, so they were able to try a number of recipes before settling on the best ones to let the customers sample.

The winners were a buttery almond biscuit coated in powdered sugar ("wedding cookies" they were called, which Mrs. Knox thought was a cute coincidence considering the whole town was excited for Keir and Alison's wedding), a spiced cookie made with treacle that was popular on the continent, and a sugar cookie cut out in the middle like a window with stained glass made from melted sweets that was sure to be a favorite of the children. They also added a dark chocolate coating to half of their ordinary shortbread biscuits and a pinch of cinnamon and nutmeg to their ginger snaps to make them stand out from Julian's.

"Now we just have to find a way to let everyone know we have something new for sale. Should we put the sign outside?"

"I have a better idea," said Charlotte.

The next day, Charlotte stood out in the street outside of Mrs. Knox's bakery with a tray in hand. Mrs. Knox had worried Charlotte would catch a chill, but she didn't mind the cold, and it was a lovely and sunny day anyway.

The samples worked even better than expected. It seemed like everyone in town came into the bakery that day, and maybe some of the visitors here for the Solstice tree lighting too, so many so that Charlotte had to abandon the samples to help Mrs. Knox keep up with the demand.

She left the tray outside, watching through the window as it continued to do its job of pulling people in while she helped the customers.

As it was nearing time to close, Charlotte headed back out to bring the tray in to wash. There, sampling one of the treacle biscuits, was Julian.

He chewed slowly, smiling to himself before seeing her and quickly wiping the crumbs from his hands. "Not bad," he said.

"Your move," she replied, taking the tray from underneath him and pulling the door shut behind her.

Chapter Nine

THE DRESS

Alison

Alison was grateful to have Rinka with her at her wedding dress appointment.

Rinka had spent the summer working with Lydiach, the green-haired fairy tailor who had made her gowns when "Lady" Rinka's had been "thrown overboard" during the pirate takeover of the Wilderise ferry. (In reality, Rinka's trunk had arrived a few weeks later unscathed, but it certainly hadn't been filled with the fine dresses the fairy tailor had made with the crown's coin.)

Which is to say that she was much better equipped to discuss dresses than Alison, who only owned about three of them. Trousers just made more sense in the city when she was commuting, and they made more sense in the country working in the garden and riding on horseback.

But a wedding was not an exercise in practicality. "It's your day," said Lydiach, flitting around on tiny white wings carrying stacks of bridal magazines and bolts of silky fabrics. "Tell me what your wildest dreams are, and I'll make them come to life."

A bold statement, but Alison would expect nothing less from a fairy. Although she knew that Lydiach and her family preferred life amongst the people, a life that meant largely abandoning public magic usage due to King Derkomai's distaste for it, Rinka had shared with her a suspicion that her gowns couldn't possibly have been made by such tiny hands in such a short time. If Lydiach used a bit of the old magic in the privacy of her workshop, she'd receive no judgment from Alison.

But Alison had no idea what her wildest dreams were, or if she did, they hadn't involved dresses that looked like they were made of whipped cream.

"Let's start with this one," said Rinka, flipping through the magazines. "Princess Chloe likes this one, and she has great taste."

The gowns within were illustrated beautifully, but to Alison, they all looked rather similar. "Ah, the lace sleeves on this one are nice," said Lydiach, pointing to a gown that looked to Alison like…well, a gown. "I have a lace like that. Let me find it for you."

The fairy flitted off again.

"This fitted waist would be nice on you," said Rinka. "You're so thin, you'll want the boning to give you some curves."

"Mmhmm," said Alison. She knew some of those words.

"What about a bias-cut satin?" said Lydiach, returning with the lace and handing it to Rinka to examine when Alison appeared uninterested. "That would accentuate her figure. Just a simple neckline—a scoop or a cowl neck, maybe."

"With some satin flowers maybe like these," said Rinka, flipping a few pages over.

"Or maybe the lace over the sleeves," said Lydiach.

"That might be too fussy for her. What about a belt? Weyland could make her a buckle or a brooch," said Rinka.

"That would really bring in the waist," said Lydiach. "Alison?"

Alison hadn't heard a word they were saying.

"Alison, are you alright?" asked Rinka. "Sorry to talk so much jargon. Do you see anything that you like?"

"I'm just...I'm a little overwhelmed," said Alison, pushing the magazines away, tears in her eyes. "I'm sorry."

There were so many decisions to make, and so many things Alison felt she was supposed to care about, but she didn't know enough about it all to even have an opinion. The only thing Alison really cared about was marrying Keir and having a nice time with their friends. All the rest of it? It was too much.

"Don't apologize, sweet girl," said Lydiach. "There's no wrong way to have a wedding."

"Let's just talk," said Rinka. "Why don't we feel the fabrics? Do you like how any of them feel?"

Alison nodded. There were delicate silks and intricate laces, fuzzy velvets and rich jacquards, fluffy tulles and gauzy chiffons, and even some rough wools that Lydiach said would be good for a cloak in case the day was very cold.

Focusing on how the fabrics felt was easier than trying to decide everything all at once. "I like the feel of this lace," said Alison. "And this one—"

"A fine chiffon," said Lydiach. "Those are lovely, but they're quite sheer. Would something like this do for the layer underneath?"

She handed Alison a very smooth silk. "Yes, that will do," said Alison.

"How do you want to look?" asked Rinka. "Prim and proper, pretty and natural, or sultry and sexy?"

Alison laughed. "I don't think sultry and sexy would do for a wedding."

"It would for a fairy wedding," said Lydiach. "You should've seen the humans' faces at my cousin's wedding. I thought one of the old ladies was going to die from shock."

"Please invite me if any of your other relatives get married. I'd love to see that," said Rinka. "So then prim and proper or pretty and natural?"

"Pretty and natural," Alison said. "Maybe if I look sort of vaguely vegetal, like I grew out of the winter woods."

"Oo, that's an idea," said Lydiach, flipping through the magazines again. She and Rinka pulled them forward a bit so Alison wouldn't have to see. They pointed and murmured quietly to each other until both were nodding in unison. "I think we know just what to do. Do you trust us?"

"I do," said Alison.

"I now pronounce you 'wedding dress decided,'" said Rinka. "You may kiss your maid of honor and talented seamstress."

Alison laughed and kissed Rinka on the cheek, thanking her for her help. She touched her finger to her lips and gently pressed it on the fairy's cheek, careful not to topple the tiny woman over.

As they left the shop, Rinka turned to Alison. "Give me the list of things you haven't decided and don't really care about. I know you don't want to burden Keir, but you don't have to do this alone."

"Well, there's the reservations at the inn for my mother and her family. There's the entertainment. Oh, and the food. And I suppose we also need to figure out if we're having it in the church…"

"Pixie's britches, Alison. Are you sure you wouldn't rather elope?"

Chapter Ten

THE LIGHTING

Charlotte

The response from Julian came on the day of the Solstice tree lighting.

Charlotte had continued giving out samples for the rest of the week, looking over to see if Julian would join her outside in response.

But as the days passed and the queue outside of Julian's shop diminished, Charlotte began to worry their strategy had been too successful. Although Charlotte was still annoyed that Julian refused to cooperate with them and had shown nothing but disdain for the notion that he should care about what happened to Mrs. Knox's shop, Charlotte didn't want to sink his business straight away either.

She needn't have worried.

The market square and High Street were bustling with foot traffic by the time Charlotte made it out with her sample tray. But few people stopped, and the ones that did took their sample and kept walking.

It couldn't have been the tree that was drawing them away. It had been fully decorated for several days, and the lighting wouldn't be until nightfall.

Charlotte noticed a crowd gathered in front of Julian's shop. But there was no Julian outside, sample tray or not.

"Come and see. It's beautiful," said Lady Sibba as Charlotte approached. The elf was wrapped in far more layers than the day required, and still she shivered as she took Charlotte by the arm, brushing her golden hair over her pointed ears to keep them covered.

Lady Sibba's graceful movements led them to the front of the crowd without incident. There, Charlotte could see what all the fuss was about.

It was a Solstice window display, although that simple description sold it short. Julian had crafted a model of the market square and High Street out of gingerbread and frosting, complete with villagers made of chocolate and licorice string lights.

And if that wasn't bad enough, the model was *moving*. The tiny villagers were walking on a loop on the powdered sugar ground. "I don't suppose it's magic," said Lady Sibba. "It doesn't feel like it, anyway."

"It's clockwork," said Julian, coming through the door to join them. He was wearing a festive green jacket today under a dark red apron, and he looked frustratingly good in it. "There's a handle to wind that sets it in motion."

"The effect is impressive," said Lady Sibba. "The painting is a nice touch as well, although next time, you should ask my Weyland to help. He's very talented."

The window to the shop had been painted with snowflakes and a continuation of the road that made it appear to go on forever. They were a bit more crudely done than the display itself, but it didn't look bad at all.

How annoying.

"Wait there. I'll show you the snow."

He winked at Charlotte before he turned to go inside, and she was embarrassed to say that it made her blush.

Julian went behind the counter and retrieved a large metal can—an icing sugar duster.

Charlotte groaned. She could see where this was going.

Julian stepped on a step ladder to the side of the display and shook the can over it, creating a sugary snowfall.

The crowd cheered.

"Great," said Charlotte. "Just what we need."

"It is," said Lady Sibba, missing Charlotte's sarcasm. "It's nice to have a new shop in town with such a committed shopkeeper. I taught him when he was in school, you know. He's a great addition to the High Street. I was just saying to Weyland the other day—"

Charlotte had started walking back to Mrs. Knox's Bakery before Lady Sibba could finish, but Lady Sibba wouldn't mind—she'd just turn to someone else to keep talking.

"What's he selling now?" said Mrs. Knox, who was waiting for Charlotte to return. The poor thing looked a bit worse for wear: they'd been pushing themselves to the limit to keep up with the sudden demand.

"I'm not sure," said Charlotte. "I didn't stay long enough to find out. He's got a Solstice display in the window. That's what's drawing the crowd. The town modeled in gingerbread."

"Oh, dear. Is it well done?"

"It is," Charlotte admitted. "He's powdering on snow for people to watch."

"It's a shame. I would have really liked that if it weren't for…" She gestured to the empty store and the counter full of Solstice biscuits. "I don't suppose we have time to put together a rival display."

It didn't make much sense to do so with Solstice only a week away. "Maybe not. But Lupercalia isn't too long after the New Year. What if we did a display for that? Little cherubs shooting arrows, turtledoves, that sort of thing."

"Oo, maybe with a wedding theme too to honor your brother and his bride."

In the end, there were so many people in Herot's Hollow that day, Julian's crowd spilled over into their shop when the queue outside became too long. They had a banner day selling biscuits, and they even received several orders from out-of-towners for delivery before Solstice, which would keep them going for the next week, at least.

"Perhaps we ought to let Julian make the Lupercalia display as well," said Mrs. Knox, counting the coin once the day was done. "I've a mind to go and thank him for the help!"

Charlotte couldn't help but wonder if the crowd into their shop may have been even larger without Julian's interference, but she didn't want to dampen Mrs. Knox's spirits.

"Are you coming to the lighting?" asked Charlotte. The crowd had moved into the square now by the sounds of it.

"Oh no, I don't think so," said Mrs. Knox. "You know I'm not fond of crowds. Not unless they're in my shop and I'm safely behind the counter."

Charlotte knew this about Mrs. Knox, but she couldn't believe she wasn't tempted by the first 'lectric lights in Herot's Hollow turning on.

She was the only one who was absent. The market square was full to the brim. Everyone had come from miles around to see the show.

A platform had been erected near the Solstice tree. Charlotte spotted Keir near the base of the platform arguing with Prince Idris.

"They know you're here. They've seen you. You don't have to say much," said Keir. "'Merry Solstice and a Happy New Year.' It isn't complicated."

"I still don't see why you can't do it. It's going to be your land."

"No, it's all going to be *your* land—"

"Would you both quit your bickering? I'm the one doing most of the talking," said Gwenla. "Unless one of you would rather?"

"No, no, by all means," said Keir, bowing slightly to the dwarf. Neither Alison nor Rinka spoke up to take the honors from Gwenla either.

"Finnli, get down!" Gwenla shouted. Finnli had begun to climb up the platform, and he was making his way towards the Solstice tree.

"But the ornament was crooked—"

"Later," said Gwenla. "It'll do for now. I don't want you up there without a ladder."

"Reminds me of someone," Keir whispered to Charlotte. She had been something of a tree climber herself, once.

"Charlotte, would you mind watching him while I'm on stage?"

Charlotte was surprised. She was frequently in charge of the resident cats, but a whole dwarf? She'd never done much child-minding when she lived with the korrigans.

"I want someone who has a chance of getting him down if he manages to get up there," said Gwenla, gesturing at the tree.

"Alright, I guess—" said Charlotte, but Gwenla was already gone.

"It's impressive how she manages that," said Alison. "She gives you a task, and before you've had a chance to argue, she's vanished."

"Truly an inspiration," said Rinka.

"She'd better be back soon," said Idris. "It's almost time to begin."

"Oh, humbug, you old misery guts. Some people like Winter Solstice," said Rinka, elbowing him in the side.

"Miss Charlotte." Finnli was tugging on the sleeve of Charlotte's work dress. She realized she should have gone home and changed for the occasion, but if she left now, she might miss it. Plus, she'd have a seven-year-old boy in tow.

"Yes, Finnli?"

"Can we go talk to Mr. Blair?"

Finnli pointed to a figure standing off on his own under an archway that led down to the river. "He looks lonely over there."

Charlotte felt for Julian in spite of everything. He had been gone for a long time, just as she had, and it could be tough to fit in again in a small village after an absence. It wasn't that the villagers weren't friendly, but people tended to get set into their ways, into their routines of who they spoke to and spent time with. She'd managed to reintegrate herself with frequent appearances down at the inn, but she hadn't seen Julian try the same approach. In fact, she hadn't seen him outside of his shop at all.

That wasn't altogether surprising. He'd have to be working long hours in the back after closing to keep up with the demands their competition had brought. But still, Charlotte felt sad to see him on his own.

But just as she'd decided to go over and speak to him, Keir took the stage.

"We'll go once it's over," she whispered to Finnli as the crowd quieted down.

"Welcome to the first annual lighting of the Solstice tree here in Herot's Hollow," said Keir. "I'm Dr. Keir Ainsley, the Marquess of Caernock, and I welcome you all to our village. I hope you'll stay and enjoy the Solstice festivities. Now allow me to introduce our most honored guest, his royal highness, Prince Idris of Loegria and Wilderise!"

Keir bowed to Prince Idris. Charlotte tried to reconcile the man before her, the dragon prince of Loegria, an imposing, devastatingly handsome man in the finest suit she'd ever seen, with the stories Keir had told her of what a ridiculous buffoon he could be.

"Thank you, thank you," said Idris, waving to the crowd as they applauded with that closed hand wave the royals always preferred. This was meant to be her brother's best man? "As you know, my father King Derkomai has a great interest in developing Wilderise and bringing this magnificent land into the modern age."

"Gods save the king!" someone shouted in the crowd.

Keir looked at Idris, confused. Hadn't he just fought with him about speaking at all? And now here he was, rambling away…

"Tonight marks the first step in that journey, a journey we will take together. We begin with the 'lectrics, courtesy of your very own industrialist, whom I'll be introducing shortly. But first, I wanted to make one more announcement."

A hush went over the crowd.

"As some of you may know, I've chosen to take a profession in addition to my royal duties. I've devoted my life to the pursuit of knowledge, and I can think of no finer place to continue that pursuit than right here in Wilderise. I'd like to announce the construction of the King's College in Wilderise, beginning this very summer between Fossholm and Gull Bay!"

A cheer went through the crowd. No one clapped louder than Lady Sibba, who seemed as though she might scream herself hoarse.

"To support the university in its mission, we will also be opening a branch of the King's Hospital in Fossholm under the supervision of your very own Marquess of Caernock, Dr. Keir Ainsley!"

This was a surprise to Charlotte. She looked at Keir, who stood near the back of the stage. His expression was difficult to read in the dim light from the streetlamps, but it seemed as though it was a surprise to him as well.

Perhaps this was what Keir had meant about Idris being a buffoon.

"To help support the continued growth of 'lectrics here in Wilderise, I'd also like to announce a new manufactory under the supervision of Yordin of the Rodaz Mountain dwarves and your very own Gwenla of Herot's Hollow! Happy Solstice to all. Looking forward to working together to build a better Wilderise in the new year. Gwenla?"

Gwenla also seemed surprised by the news, but she concealed it better. "Welcome, everyone, to Herot's Hollow!" The crowd was still murmuring about Idris's news. He stepped forward again and held up a hand, which silenced them almost immediately. "Thank you," said Gwenla. "We're here today to mark a new beginning for Herot's Hollow, and indeed, all of Wilderise. I never thought I'd be the one stood before you. I am here because I love this town."

There were quite a few cheers at that.

"I love this place. When I heard about the plans for it, the only thing I could think of was to find a way to preserve our home. And with the help of some very clever friends, we've done it, and we've brought 'lectrics too!"

There were many more cheers now.

"The 'lectrics that will light this tree came from the sun. The very sun that grows our crops. It's good, clean 'lectricity, and no one's house had to go to the bottom of a lake for it!"

There were a few scattered cheers from the Herot's Hollow villagers, and a lot of confused murmurs from everyone else.

"Anyway, enough from me. Let's see the lights! Count down with me in five – four – three – two – one—"

Gwenla flipped a brass switch in a box at the front of the stage.

And nothing happened.

There was a collective groan from the crowd. "Wait! Wait!" shouted Gwenla. "The wire was a bit loose. Let's try it again."

She flipped the switch again, and this time, a string of lights from the streetlamp to the tree's base came on.

"Is that it?" yelled an older woman.

"No, no, hang on. Hang on, folks, we're still working out the kinks."

Finnli led Charlotte up to the stage as Alison and Rinka tried to work out what to do.

"Magic?" suggested Rinka.

"I don't know if I could pull it off," said Alison. "Idris?"

"Now wait, all of you," said Gwenla. "This ought to work. Some of the lights are working."

They followed the string of lights with their eyes to the base of the tree. "Is a wire loose there?" asked Charlotte.

"I know what's wrong," said Alison. "It happened in the street near my office. One of the bulbs is bad. Gwenla, did they send any spares?"

"There was a box with a dozen or so bulbs without any string. It's under the stage. I didn't know what to do with it."

Alison led the charge, retrieving one of the extra lightbulbs and heading to the base of the tree to switch it out. Charlotte led Finnli back to their spot in front of the stage.

"Alright, let's try this one more time. In three – two – one—"

A gasp went through the crowd. The Solstice tree in its forty-foot glory shone like the sun in the market square, the lights reflecting on the silver ornaments and twinkling in the tinsel like diamonds.

There was a slow, awed applause that built into a cheer that went on and on.

"We've done it!" yelled Gwenla. She pulled everyone she could find into a celebratory hug. When she reached Charlotte, she pulled her in too. "I'm so glad you're here, love," she whispered to her.

Charlotte looked out at the crowd behind Gwenla. There were so many people here, all of them brought together to celebrate the holiday. Everyone had someone.

Everyone except Julian.

"Come on," said Finnli. "It's lit now. Can we go see Mr. Blair?"

"Let's go," said Charlotte. Gwenla was busy greeting all the well-wishers. Charlotte was sure she wouldn't mind her watching Finnli a bit longer.

"Mr. Blair!" yelled Finnli as they approached Julian. "Would you do the coin trick again?"

Julian looked much more joyful in the glow of the new 'lectric lights. He smiled broadly at Finnli. "One more time. Then I'm going to have to find a new trick, or you might think me a one-trick pony."

"I think you're a human, not a pony," said Finnli.

"There's no fooling you," said Julian. "Alright, there's nothing in my hand."

Julian held up his hand and turned it over, showing nothing concealed.

"But there's something here behind your ear," he said, reaching behind Finnli's left ear and retrieving a silver coin, which he tossed to Finnli.

Finnli squealed. "How do you do that? Is it magic? Will you show me?"

"A sleight of hand, but I can't reveal my tricks in front of an audience." He gestured to Charlotte then pulled Finnli in conspiratorially. "Come by my shop next week," he whispered loud enough for Charlotte to hear.

"Okay," Finnli whispered back even louder. Then he spotted something beyond Julian's shoulder. "Hey, Michael! Want to play coin flip?" Finnli ran off in the direction of a human child.

"Don't go too far," called Charlotte. Finnli waved back, staying just within sight at the edge of the crowd.

"I think he stole your silver," said Charlotte to Julian.

"He'll bring it back. He's a good lad."

"What do you think of it?" asked Charlotte, gesturing to the Solstice tree.

"It's not my first time seeing the lights. But they never had a tree that big in Arcas Dyrne, not even at City Hall. Not even at the castle."

"You've been to the king's Solstice festival?"

"Just the once," said Julian. "Last year, before my father was released. I was in a festive mood."

Charlotte already knew how that had turned out for him. "And now? Has coming out here gone as you hoped?"

Julian shifted his weight, considering how to answer. "In some ways, yes. The village has taken to the shop like I hoped they would. But I'll admit that there are things I didn't see coming."

Charlotte felt her pulse quicken. Perhaps he was coming to his senses at last. Perhaps he was beginning to see the harm he was causing the bakery, beginning to consider what he might do to end the feud. "Like?"

"Like you," said Julian.

Well, that was fair enough. Not what Charlotte was hoping to hear, but it was fair.

"I never thought I'd see you again. There was a time when I hoped for it. When they didn't find your…body. I went looking myself, you know."

"I didn't know that." Charlotte had seen many of the people searching for her, the korrigan's magic helping her blend into the riverbank and the woods. But she had never seen Julian among them.

"It was after all the official searches stopped. Father wouldn't let me join them; I think he was afraid of what I might see, and now that I'm older, I don't blame him for that. But I knew you were a good swimmer. I'd swam in that same river with you a dozen times. I told my father I was going to school, and then I crept past the schoolhouse and went down to the river. I told Lady Sibba I'd been ill. It took about a week before they caught on to me."

"You went every day?"

Julian laughed. "I wasn't the best at avoiding getting caught. You were better at that, from what I recall."

Mostly true, although Charlotte had plenty of missteps of her own. "I never saw you."

"But you were close. You were nearby, weren't you?"

"Probably," said Charlotte. "The korrigans tend to stay near that part of the river, although they do move to the lake and beyond at times. But I might have been nearby."

Julian looked up, unable to look Charlotte in the eye. "I liked to think you were nearby. Hey." He pointed to something green near the top of the archway. "Is that mistletoe?"

The breath caught in Charlotte's lungs. There was a spark of something between them, rivalry or not. There was a history, a friendship deep and pure that had been lurking under the surface, ready to resume at the first opportunity. Charlotte had tried to reject the feeling once she learned of Julian's plans, but it tugged at her, willing her to look upwards into Julian's eyes.

They were soft and filled with the sparking reflections of the Solstice lights. Charlotte felt the pull of them, saw the tilt of Julian's head, the lean in, the warmth of his body near hers.

She leaned too, gave into the urge for a moment. They could argue about the shop later. She could find a way to get him to come around. It didn't matter right now. It was a nice night, a nice moment—

Finnli crashed into Charlotte's legs. "Ow! Oh! Miss Ainsley. I'm sorry Miss Ainsley. Ow!"

"Are you alright?" asked Charlotte, feeling the earth return under her feet along with the throbbing of her knee. The dwarf boy was on the ground rubbing his elbow.

"Mmhmm," said Finnli, his little mouth set into a line, his eyes full of tears.

"Let's see it." Charlotte took a look at his elbow—not a mark on it, but she bet it hurt nonetheless. Her knee surely did. "You're a brave little soldier. You'll be alright."

Finnli nodded and slowly stood. "We lost the coin," he said to Julian.

"What are you talking about?" asked Julian. "It's right here."

Julian plucked another silver from behind Finnli's ear, returning the smile to his face.

Charlotte's heart fluttered and flipped in her chest.

If she hadn't been in trouble before, she was in trouble now.

Chapter Eleven

THE SOLSTICE PARTY

Alison

The night of the Solstice lighting had been chaotic but incredible.

Alison worried that the out-of-town visitors would panic at the sight of the spriggan, but she didn't want him to be excluded when he'd been so critical to procuring the tree. An hour before dusk, she had led him up the side of the church to the tower where he'd hung on, doing his best impression of a vine.

It was a little unnerving—Alison was still a bit touchy where vines were concerned—but it had worked. No one seemed any the wiser about the spriggan's presence, but he had been able to see the spectacle firsthand.

Once the crowd had gone, she led him into the square to see the tree up close.

"Remarkable," he said. "Like little bursts of sunlight at nighttime. And look how it shines on the jewelry. I would like to have one of those jewels one day."

The ornaments on the Solstice tree were too big for the spriggan to wear in his ordinary form, but Alison had taken him to the forge to see if Strelka had any smaller ones to give away from her practice attempts.

They were in luck: there was a box of gold and silver ornaments meant for the much smaller tree that usually occupied the market square. The spriggan chose a silver ornament and hung it from the side of his head, roughly where Strelka wore her earrings.

"How does it look?" asked the spriggan.

"Very festive," said Alison.

⁘

The week before Winter Solstice offered Alison a welcome reprieve from the turmoil of wedding planning.

Having already sorted her Solstice gifts, she welcomed the chance to wrap them in peace while the others frantically completed preparations for the day.

"I've never had so much time to get things done before," she told Willow as she wrapped a tiny bow around the small box that held Keir's present. "I was never able to take more than a day or two off from number-crunching. It's a busy time at year end. I was always the one rushing around the shops at the last minute, buying whatever they had left with little thought to how it would be received."

"That sounds awful," said Willow. She was lounging in a bed Alison had made from a wicker basket and a thick tartan blanket close enough to the fire to feel its warmth, but not so close as to singe her lovely fur.

"It was awful," said Alison. "But it was the only way to get by."

Keir still wasn't back from checking in on his patients by the time she had finished, so she retrieved the poetry book and set about filling in some of the blank pages.

"I feel like I haven't written enough about summer. What's your favorite thing about summer, Willow?"

Willow scrunched her tabby brow, thinking hard. "Dragonflies," she said, finally. "They're the absolute best to chase. They often manage to bring a fish to the surface when they land in the water. It's double the treats."

Alison wasn't sure about the relatability of fishing with live dragonflies as bait, but chasing insects in summer might do more generally. "Thanks."

"Did you write anything about the wedding yet?"

Alison shook her head. "My poems aren't that personal."

"Why not?"

"I don't know. I don't think my poems are good enough for all that." Alison had written poetry inspired by events in her life, but nothing that intimate.

"Then you're not going to write something for the wedding?"

Alison laughed. "The last thing I want to do at my wedding is force everyone to listen to something I wrote. We're there to celebrate our marriage, not to listen to me ramble."

"If you say so. But you've never written anything for Keir? Or about him?"

"I love him too much to do that to him."

Willow hopped out of the basket and onto Alison's desk. She sat in front of Alison, staring at her with big green eyes. "I wish you wouldn't do that. Your poetry isn't bad, you know."

"You're my worst critic! I don't think I've ever written a line that you liked the first time."

"That's not true. I like plenty of your lines. And if anything, I'm your second worst critic."

Alison was beginning to get annoyed with the cat. "How much poetry have you read anyway?"

Willow turned away from Alison. "Lady Willana liked poetry. She used to read it to Gwenla. So alright, I haven't read any, but I've heard plenty."

"Oh, Willow. I'm sorry," said Alison. She was quite embarrassed at her outburst. "I just get a little sensitive about the poetry. I didn't mean to be rude." She held out her hand, and Willow allowed her to give her conciliatory chin scratches.

"Well, all I was trying to say is that you don't need to be so sensitive. You have a talent."

"I appreciate that. It's nice to hear it but harder to make myself believe it."

"I didn't mean to push you. I know you have a lot on your plate as it is with the wedding."

With Rinka around to share some of the planning duties, Alison did have a bit of time back. Perhaps it wouldn't be a terrible thing to write something for the wedding. Not a poem necessarily, that felt a bit trite. But something a bit more raw. Something she could share with Keir from the heart.

"You know what? You're right," said Alison, retrieving one of the blank pages. "I've never been fond of those stuffy old Unified Pantheon vows anyway. I'll give it a go."

Willow purred and rubbed against her hand, scratching a stray line on the page.

"Sorry," said Willow, looking at the mark. "Just helping you get started."

⚛

On Solstice morning, Keir gently woke Alison just after dawn.

"Happy Solstice, my darling," he said, bringing her a cup of tea in bed. They had spent the night at his house; they were heading to Gwenla's house for lunch and needed to bring some of Keir's chairs in order for everyone to have a place to sit. Keir was already shaved and dressed, and next to him on the bed, there was a small giftbox.

"Aren't we going to exchange gifts with the others?" asked Alison. She had taken his gift to Gwenla's with the rest the day before.

"My gift to you is a bit sentimental. I thought you might like the chance to open it in private."

Alison studied the box as Keir handed it to her—it was small, roughly the same size as the one she'd used for Keir's gift. Jewelry, perhaps?

She tugged on the string and removed the wrapping.

Inside the box was a small golden pendant in the shape of an oval. It had a floral filigree not unlike the ring she had chosen for Keir. "Weyland made this?"

Keir nodded. "Open it."

Alison turned over the pendant, seeing the tiny hinges and realizing it was a locket. "It's not the cursed one, right?"

"No," Keir laughed. "No, I didn't raid Idris's cursed objects closet for anything other than the ring, and I only did that because you loved it so much. The locket is one of Weyland's creations, although how he was able to create something so delicate with those hands of his—"

"Oh," said Alison, opening the locket.

Inside was a picture of her late father. He was young in the picture; it must have been taken when Alison was just a little girl.

"I wrote to your mother for it. I thought you'd like to have something of his at the wedding. Something you could keep with you, close to your heart."

Tears sprang to Alison's eyes. "Thank you," she said softly.

Keir held her as she gently cried. "I'm sorry he can't be there with us," he said, stroking her dark hair.

"He would've loved you," said Alison. She was certain of that. Though it was incredibly difficult to go through such an important time in her life without him, it was a comfort to know he would've loved the person she had chosen.

When her tears had calmed, Alison looked at the empty frame on the left side of the locket. An idea struck her. "Are there any pictures of your mother? I'd like to have her with us as well."

"I'd like that too," said Keir, clearly touched by the gesture. "I'll take a look when we're at the manor for New Year's."

Keir helped Alison put the locket on after she had dressed. The gold was lovely against the dark green of her Solstice dress, and it felt so good to carry a bit of her father with her wherever she went.

⚜

Alison, Keir, and Charlotte were the first to arrive at Gwenla's gathering.

"Finnli, be a good lad and help them with the chairs," said Gwenla. "I've got to go check on the roast. Will you help yourselves to some wine? The kettle's on if you'd rather have tea. Oh, and Charlotte—the brandy's in the cupboard with the fruitcake."

With Keir and Charlotte's additions, Gwenla's cozy living room was full to the bursting with gifts. It was full to the bursting, period: the little brown couch was covered in red pillows, all of them handstitched, and there was a great pile of knitted blankets in the corner.

(Not that they were needed: the fire roared in Gwenla's ancient hearth.)

Dinah and Willow were missing; Alison was surprised not to find them by the fire. But then she heard Dinah's meows from the kitchen. "No roast for you, troublesome girls!" said Gwenla.

"But really Gwenla, it does smell so nice," said Willow in her silkiest, most persuasive voice. "Surely one little bite wouldn't hurt us."

"You'll have your bite when we eat and not a moment before it."

There was a knocking at the door.

"Alison, could you get that?" called Gwenla from the kitchen.

Alison greeted Rinka and Idris, who had arrived by carriage. "I hope you don't mind the indulgence. The gifts were a bit…heavy," said Rinka.

The carriage driver began unloading box after huge box from the back of the carriage.

"I don't know where all of that is going to fit—" began Alison, but Idris had already begun to rearrange the great gift pile to make room.

"Are Lady Sibba and Weyland coming?" asked Rinka, gesturing to a pair of gifts.

"They're keeping to themselves this morning," said Alison. "They said they might pop 'round later."

"Did you invite Julian?" Keir asked Charlotte.

Charlotte blushed. "No. I wasn't sure it was a good idea, with the rivalry and all."

"Rivalry?" asked Rinka. Charlotte filled her and Idris in on the rival bake shop.

"That's easily managed," said Idris. "Keir, just evict him. Your father won't even notice."

Alison hadn't realized that Lord Ainsley likely owned the building Julian was renting.

Charlotte apparently hadn't either, judging by her surprised expression. "You can't do that," she said. "He needs the shop to survive."

"Wait, are we for or against the rival bake shop?" asked Rinka.

"It's a cheese shop," said Charlotte. "We don't want him to leave. We just want him to stop baking things and stealing business from Mrs. Knox."

"Ah," said Rinka. "Thank you. Now that I know how we feel about it, I'm ready to do whatever it takes to help...stop the baker from baking. Or the cheese monger from baking? Is that right?"

"Close enough," said Charlotte.

"Gwenla, can I help you in the kitchen?" asked Alison.

"No, no, no, it's done. Sit down. We'll all fit around the table if we squeeze."

Gwenla had installed the leaf in her dining table, filling up the entirety of the room. The table was already set with six places; the smaller kitchen table had been set up for Finnli and the cats in the kitchen.

Over Gwenla's protests, Alison helped carry in bowls of roasted sprouts and spiced squash, a gravy boat, and the largest pan of mashed potatoes she'd ever seen. Gwenla brought in a tray of puffy golden pastries cooked from the fat of the roast, and then she brought in the star of the show: the roast itself.

It was a beautiful cut of beef, nice and brown on the outside, delicately pink and tender on the inside. The entire spread was so lovely it was difficult to tear it apart in order to eat it.

Difficult, but not impossible.

"Shall we have a Solstice toast for the chef?" asked Alison once they had all served themselves. "To Gwenla, champion of Herot's Hollow. May her days be long and bright."

"May her days be long and bright. Cheers!" they said in unison.

"Shall we also toast the prince?" said Gwenla. "It's a first, having royalty at my table."

"Absolutely not," said Idris, setting his glass down. "If we keep toasting, the food will be cold."

Gwenla laughed. "A fair point. Very well. Happy Solstice, all! Dig in!"

After lunch, they gathered in the crowded living room to exchange gifts.

Gwenla received a number of gifts for her garden, including a nice new pair of secateurs from Alison and Keir and some rare bulbs from the continent ordered by Rinka and Idris. "Oh, what lovely daffodils!" said Gwenla, holding up the package to show everyone the illustration. "If I plant them right away, they'll be up by Lupercalia."

Charlotte received a special baking pan from Gwenla for making cheesecakes. "If Julian insists on selling pastries, you might as well try selling something cheesy."

Everyone had brought toys and games for Finnli, who had grown up with many siblings and wasn't used to receiving more than one gift. "I don't know what to play with first," he said, quite overwhelmed. In the end, he chose a puzzle and started a war with the cats to keep the pieces off the floor, much to his delight.

Alison had gotten Keir cufflinks made by Weyland to wear at the wedding. "I'm sorry they aren't quite as meaningful as your present," she said. Keir had reassured her that they were lovely, and he was kind enough to put them on right away to prove how much he liked them.

No one had known what to get Idris. Alison had gone down to the archive and asked Duncan Corbett (who would be attending her wedding with Nigel Smalls after all, a great bit of gossip) to copy all the stories of local curses and their remedies into a pamphlet. Alison had worried Idris would find it overly practical as a gift, but he had been thrilled. "There are some unique stories here," said Idris as he skimmed through it. "You know, it wouldn't be a bad project, going from town to town, collecting their curse lore. Thank you for the idea as well."

But the winner of the day was Rinka. Idris's gift to her had come in a huge box he'd struggled to carry into Gwenla's living room, and Rinka had struggled to even open it. "What did you get me, a horse?"

In the end, Gwenla had to find a crowbar to break into the crate.

"I don't believe it," said Rinka as she lifted something round from within it. It was a metal wheel about a foot wide, and wrapped around it was something dark that Alison didn't recognize. "Are all of these— how many are there? Is this every picture show that's ever been made?"

Rinka was practically yelling; she was so excited. Alison remembered how it used to scare the Halfling Mr. Theo in their building in Arcas Dyrne when she spoke too loudly. They had come a long way since then.

"It's every picture show I could manage to find," said Idris.

"But how are we meant to watch them? They need a projector to run them, and 'lectrics to run the projector. Oh, this one is so cute! It's a little fairy princess story," she said, holding up another one of the reels that must have somehow held picture shows.

"There's a projector waiting at Weldan House." Idris smiled at Keir—they'd clearly planned this surprised together.

"Gwenla, everyone, you must come with us back to Weldan House," said Rinka. "We can send you home in a carriage tonight. I have to show you all of my favorites."

"Aunt Gwenla, can we go? Please? I want to see the pictures," said Finnli. "We only get dwarf pictures under the mountain."

"Let me do some washing up first," said Gwenla.

"Sit down," said Alison. "I'll do that."

"No, I insist—"

"You can supervise from the kitchen table," said Keir, joining Alison in clearing the plates.

Gwenla sat uncomfortably at her kitchen table as Keir and Alison washed the dishes. "You really don't have to—"

"Please, Gwenla. Let us do something. You must have been up all night making all of this," said Alison.

"And it was worth it," said Keir. "It was a wonderful meal."

Gwenla finally sat back in her chair. Alison glanced back to look at her and saw she was smiling and nodding. "What would Lady Willana have said?" she asked, recognizing Gwenla's look when she was imagining their conversation.

"She would have loved this. Nothing would have made her happier than to see everyone together again. To see the house full of laughter. She would have been so proud of you both."

"She would have been proud of you too, Gwenla," said Keir. "You made this all possible."

"We all did," said Gwenla. "Together."

Chapter Twelve

NEW YEAR'S EVE

Rinka

Rinka regretted agreeing to host the New Year's celebration for Wilderise's Hill Country at Weldan House.

It wasn't that she didn't enjoy parties. She loved them, in fact, and she was looking forward to a night of dancing and revelry. It wasn't even that she minded planning, although there was a lot to organize between the decorations, the catering, and the entertainment. It was good practice for Alison's wedding, after all, and she'd been able to make some useful contacts with the help of the Weldan House staff (while keeping quiet about the upcoming nuptials in order to prevent Lord Ainsley finding out).

No, the problem was the picture-show projector. All that planning and organizing took time away from enjoying the best gift anyone had ever given her.

Rinka managed to find time at night after approving the napkin selection and listening to the string quartet rehearse to watch some of the pictures in the Weldan House ballroom, the second room in the house to have its 'lectrics completed.

There were shows she'd never seen before and shows she thought she'd never see again. Once a picture show left the small theatre near the butcher shop, it seldom came back again.

Idris hadn't really gotten it at first, but even he enjoyed a spooky picture with a vampire that turned into a bat.

"I think Professor Marin would find that offensive," said Idris. The professor had been critical in their creation of the solar generators which rested in a field outside, the power-savers she had helped them design keeping the 'lectricity flowing to the projector even at night.

She was also a vampire. "Do you know she can't turn into a bat? Did you ever ask her?" asked Rinka. "Maybe she'd be offended to find out you doubted her."

"I'll make sure to ask her when I return to Winwold next week."

Rinka pouted, her lower lip covering her fangs. "Must you really return so soon? The term doesn't start for a couple of weeks."

"If I'm to be out for a week at Lupercalia, I have to leave plans for my classes. Why, will you miss me?" Idris moved a bit closer to Rinka on the couch they'd pulled into the center of the ballroom, the best view of the screen they'd made of a sheet hung from a curtain rod.

Rinka snorted. "Of course I'll miss you." They hadn't been apart since the summer.

"Good. I like to be missed."

She shoved him away.

"Hey. You can always come back with me, you know."

"Alison needs me here," said Rinka, and it was really true. Alison was so clever, but she had no idea how to throw a good party. Rinka was grateful the generator income meant she could stay as long as she liked without needing to work. In fact, if she had her way, she'd spend the rest of her days planning parties and would never work a day again. "But will you miss *me?*" she asked.

"More than anything," said Idris, soft and low, in a way that made Rinka forget about the picture-show.

⊷⊙⊙⊶

The New Year's ball was the best one Rinka had ever been to.

After a summer rubbing elbows with the wealthiest and most betitled (and entitled) of Loegria and Wilderise, Rinka felt a return to her roots was in order: she asked Keir if they could invite absolutely everyone to the ball, and he agreed.

Rinka arranged for carriage service to bring anyone who wanted to attend from the nearby villages and farms to and from Weldan House. Most of the people had attended parties and festivals on the Weldan House lawn, but few had been invited inside before.

The Weldan House staff were somewhat more reluctant to open their house to the entire region than Lord Ainsley's heir, although many of them had long taken the position that what Lord Ainsley didn't know wouldn't hurt him. Still, if they pushed back on allowing the children of the guests to sleep in the drawing room or on moving the pianoforte into the ballroom to accompany the quartet, Rinka only needed to ask Idris to step in and insist. As infuriating as it was, his rank did tend to open many doors.

It all paid off in the end. The ball was a smashing success. Rinka had never seen a happier crowd, people of all shapes and sizes and from every walk of life dressed in their finest, enjoying a moment free of troubles. A moment to celebrate their hard work and to begin the New Year with hope and joy.

The best part of the night would be the last, but the second-best part was introducing Wilderise to the picture show. Rinka had chosen a special favorite for the occasion: a pirate picture that reminded her of meeting Idris.

She thought she'd have to coax him into telling the tale for the crowd, but Idris was caught up in the jubilation too. He launched into the story they'd told the magazine unbidden, reluctantly omitting the magic in the telling.

"It was a shame you couldn't mention the sword or the boat," said Rinka to him after the picture show was finished. "I bet they would have lost it if you brought out the sword."

Idris flipped the coin he used in his pocket. "Trying not to antagonize Father until the university is built. Once it's finished, though…"

"You'll singlehandedly bring magic back into style?"

Idris gave her a look that said, *you think I couldn't?* "There's too much opportunity in it to ignore. Think of the generators. What else could be created if we stopped thinking of magic and science as two separate ventures?"

"A purely practical endeavor, of course, and in no way tied to your desire to show off."

"You're the one that said I should." Idris pulled the coin from his pocket and turned it into a silver swan. It flapped its wings and hovered between them.

Rinka stood in front of it, blocking the crowd from seeing it. It was really quite amazing. As much as she liked to tease Idris about his arrogance, she had to admit it was pretty well deserved.

"Fine, yes, you're very impressive, and I want everyone else to see how impressive you are. Are you happy?"

"Yes," said Idris, putting his hand on the small of her back and kissing her cheek. "Very."

As the night wound towards midnight, Rinka spied her friends from Herot's Hollow making their way to the balcony to see the fireworks.

"Rinka, over here!" called Alison. "Where's Idris?"

He had been right behind her, but when Rinka looked back, he'd vanished. "Probably off to get some sparkling wine for the midnight toast."

"He better hurry. The countdown will start any minute," said Keir, checking his pocket watch.

A bonfire had been lit out on the lawn below, and most of the guests gathered around it for warmth as they waited for the show to begin. Rinka waited for

Idris near the railing of the balcony, rubbing her bare arms and wishing she could join the crowd by the fire.

But someone had to lead the countdown, and if Idris didn't show up soon, it might have to be her.

"Are we ready?" asked Idris, suddenly appearing from seemingly nowhere. He panted a bit, his shoulders heaving as if he'd just been running.

"Nearly there," said Keir. "Get ready…steady…" Then he held up his hand. "Ten…nine…"

The others joined in, drawing the attention of the crowd below. "Eight…seven…"

The crowd cheered and joined in too. "Six…five…four…"

Idris wrapped his arm around Rinka's waist. There was something in his hand.

"Three…two…one. Happy New Year!"

Right on queue, the fireworks erupted from near the river. They filled the sky with sparkles in red, white, green, gold, and blue.

It was magnificent. Rinka cheered with the crowd and then turned to Idris, remembering the fireworks from the summer.

He was down on one knee.

"Rinka—" he began, but she screamed, interrupting him.

"Oh my Gods," said Alison from beside her, pulling Keir's arm to turn him around to look.

"Rinka—"

Rinka jumped up and down, fine gown be damned. "Really? Really?"

She hugged Alison. She looked up at the fireworks. She screamed again.

"Rinka—"

She fanned her face; her grey skin was going red from the flush of surprise. Her eyes had filled with tears.

She looked down at Idris, blinking the tears away.

Gods, she loved this man. He was such an idiot. He was so wonderfully absurd, such an incredible contradiction of chaos and authority and magic and silliness. He was the dark beauty of midnight as much as he was sunlight on a summer day. He would be the most powerful man in the world one day, perhaps, and Rinka would be his queen.

An orc for a queen. What an idea.

Rinka had barely let herself consider it before. Even after the summer had ended and it had become clear to her that there was more to them than just a passing fancy, she never truly thought it would last.

But Idris made anything feel possible. She knew she would never fit into high society. She had the skill to please a crowd, sure, but she could not fool herself. She would always be a common orc at heart.

But Idris made her feel like that was enough.

"Rinka," said Idris once she had finally stopped squealing. "When you came crashing into my life, I could not have imagined how much you would change it. You have given me hope where I had none. You have given me purpose and strengthened my convictions. You have healed old wounds and taught me how to care. You have brightened all my days, so much so that my entire world looks dim without you.

"I don't know what I can offer you. I know you care deeply about this world, and I know you want to see it better. I believe completely in your ability to do so by yourself, but if you'll have me, I would go to the ends of the earth to help you. I would do anything for you. I am yours to command."

Rinka lost the ability to breathe. She had never heard Idris speak so sincerely for so long. Both of them usually cut through moments like this with a joke, something to stop the show of vulnerability, to hide away the deep and serious feelings where they would be safe.

She let the moment pass, let the words hang there between them. Real, genuine words with no jest or caveat or pretense.

Idris looked up at her, the fireworks reflected in his dark eyes. "Will you be my wife?"

"Of course," she said, letting him place a simple ring with a large red stone (very large, Gods, what a rock) on her ring finger as he trembled.

"Really?" asked Idris now, not sure if he believed her.

"Yes!" said Rinka, throwing her arms around him as Alison and Keir cheered.

And then, because she simply could not make it one more moment without saying something silly, she added, "All hail Princess Rinka!"

"Princess Rinka!" said Alison, toasting her with a glass of sparkling wine Idris must have asked the Weldan House staff to bring around.

"All hail the Princess!" said Idris, holding up her hand. The crowd below was too busy kissing and toasting and cheering to notice.

Rinka took advantage of their distraction to sneak in a New Year's kiss of her own with her new fiancé as the fireworks burst through the air around them.

It was magical.

Chapter Thirteen

DÉTENTE?

Charlotte

There was an art to piping frosting that Charlotte hadn't quite managed to master.

It was two weeks after the New Year and less than a month until Keir and Alison's wedding and the celebration of Lupercalia, and though Charlotte had practiced every single day since the Solstice, her loops and swirls still looked as though a child had done them.

She held up a heart-shaped cake she'd been using to practice, showing Mrs. Knox her lack of progress. "You might as well hire Finnli at this rate. I'm pretty sure he could do a better job."

Charlotte had thought of Finnli and the moment he'd interrupted a few weeks earlier often. She was grateful to the boy: he'd stopped her from doing something impulsive that would have been both a betrayal to Mrs. Knox and a terrible complication in whatever fledgling friendship or rivalry she was forming with Julian.

And yet her mind often wandered back to the moment, lingering on what might have happened if Finnli hadn't been there at all…

"This side is an improvement," said Mrs. Knox, pointing to the first bit of piping Charlotte had done. "You just need to have patience. Take breaks if your hands hurt. See how this line is uneven? That's because you've rushed it and tried to use the bottom of the bag. Always make sure you have enough frosting made up for the entire cake before you begin. It's difficult to match the color after the fact—see how this pink is a little too dark?"

Charlotte could see all of the mistakes clearly enough without Mrs. Knox pointing them out, but she thanked her for the tips. She knew the baker was right, but she hated that it took so long to improve.

She wished she'd had more time to practice, but they'd spent most of the previous weeks planning and executing the Lupercalia display in the window.

It was quite a lovely scene. They'd modeled the interior of the church in sugar cookies and chocolates, and they'd hung turtle doves and hearts on thin silken threads that swayed when the door opened. Charlotte had even made the wedding cakes in miniature—she had found it was a lot easier to decorate them when they were smaller than her hand.

Charlotte looked past the display and across the street at Julian's window. He'd taken down his Solstice display shortly after New Year's, but so far, he hadn't answered their challenge with a Lupercalia display of his own.

In fact, it had been a couple of days since Charlotte had seen much of a crowd at Julian's store.

"Do you think he's finally given it up?" Charlotte asked Mrs. Knox. "The bread seems to have been going more quickly, and the croissants too. The coffee has certainly been helping, but I wonder if that's all."

"I was just wondering that myself," said Mrs. Knox. "Did you want to go find out?"

Charlotte nodded, setting off for the cheese shop that might actually be a cheese shop now. The day was bitterly cold; Charlotte slammed the door behind her as she entered, trying to keep out the chill.

Julian was leaning over the counter. He was as handsome as ever—Charlotte pictured him under the mistletoe on Solstice, his face inches from hers. She pictured him coming out from behind the counter and pulling her into a kiss.

She blushed, shoving the thought from her mind. It was clear to see from his posture that this wasn't the same Julian who'd so kindly entertained Finnli, who'd come so close to taking her in his arms…

This Julian barely lifted his head to greet her. "Come to gloat, have you?"

Charlotte didn't understand. "What do you mean? Do you mean you've given up the baking idea after all?"

"Not by choice," said Julian. "I'm out of sugar and yeast, and my supplier can't get any to me for another week at least."

There wasn't much you could bake without one or both of those things. Some muffins, maybe. Sourdough, though that required a starter, something Julian likely didn't have.

Of course, Mrs. Knox had some starter she could share, and she had plenty of sugar and yeast besides.

But Charlotte could see why Julian hadn't asked. "Will you manage without it?"

"The wine moves well enough on its own," said Julian. "I guess we're going to find out if it's enough."

Charlotte bristled at his attitude. "You know, you could have come to Mrs. Knox for help instead of making an enemy of her. If you were worried the shop wouldn't do well, you could have asked what you could do to make it succeed. The people around here would have helped you out. Keir might have helped you on the rent. Alison and Weyland would have made you fliers. Hells, if you'd told Gwenla what you needed, she would have personally escorted every person in town in here and held the door shut until they bought something. That's what it's like here. You said you moved here because you were happy here, but it doesn't seem like you understand this place at all."

"I don't need help," said Julian, straightening his back and pulling himself upright. "I've never had help, and I've always gotten by. That's what you don't understand. I thought maybe you'd get it because you had to strike out on your own even before I did, but you clearly don't understand. I'll find a way to manage, with or without the baking. I don't need your pity."

The last words were so biting, it left Charlotte feeling as though she had been thrown out even though he hadn't made a move towards her.

"Fine," said Charlotte, feeling the heat rise into her face. "You won't have it. And you won't have my help. Good luck, Julian. You're going to need it."

She slammed the door again on the way out, this time glad to be on the other side of it.

Chapter Fourteen

JITTERS

Keir

It was the darkest part of the night as Keir left Foss-holm on horseback.

It seemed to be a rule of complicated pregnancies that the baby always finally came in the middle of the night or on a holiday or right when the doctor had sat down for tea. But the baby—half elf, half human in this case, a combination that sometimes posed a challenge for the smaller hips of the elf mother—had come with little incident, though she did take her time coming.

Keir led his horse through the Fossholm High Street, stopping to admire the new 'lectric lights that lined the way to the frozen lake beyond. This was what progress looked like, the good kind of it. He'd treated the pixies who lit the lamps in Herot's Hollow for burns countless times. Now they were responsible for changing the bulbs once they burnt out, a much less dangerous task.

Keir was less certain about the benefits of the manufactory. He had seen the injuries in his time studying medicine in Arcas Dyrne. Lacerations, amputations, severe burns, broken limbs. Sometimes in children barely old enough to hold a wrench, let alone work an assembly line.

It wasn't that Keir doubted Idris, but he knew the prince shared a bit of his father's penchant for jumping on new ideas without giving enough attention to the details needed to see them through. But Idris's flights of fancy were far less destructive than King Derkomai's, thank the Gods, and with Rinka at his side and Gwenla leading the manufactory charge, he knew they'd do what they could to keep the good people of Wilderise safe from harm.

With any luck, the hospital would be so little used he'd have to shut it down.

Keir peered out over the ice to the eastern shore where the hospital would stand. It was a short ride from Weldan House, his and Alison's eventual home, but it was a longer trip back to Herot's Hollow. The town he'd turned his back on had come to mean so much to him since Alison had arrived, and he knew it meant so much to Alison as well.

Could she be happy here in Fossholm? Could she be happy in Weldan House, in its cavernous halls and palatial grounds? She'd come to love tending the little garden in her hedge maze. Would she feel the same telling a team of gardeners what to plant?

And what of being the duchess? If Keir continued practicing medicine, and he couldn't picture giving it up now, would she be content to host balls and festivals even in his absence? To go to court when called?

Was this the life she wanted for herself, or was it something Keir was imposing on her by virtue of who he was? Who he had been born to be, whether he wanted it or not.

He was terrified to ask her, he realized. Selfishly, he wanted her with him no matter what she wanted. She was such a comfort to him. She made him better.

But was that fair to her? What did he offer her? What could he give her that would make the sacrifices she would need to make worthwhile?

Keir rode through the darkened woods along the road to Herot's Hollow, lost in contemplation.

He didn't notice the fairy fire until it was right on top of him.

"If it isn't the finest dancer in Wilderise," said a familiar voice.

It was a good thing Genn had spoken. Keir never would have recognized the fairy from their figure alone in the light of the fairy fire. Genn was an eighth of the size from when Keir had seen them last, but it was the same fairy—same blue hair, same white wings, same human features. Same mischief.

"I didn't know you could leave the place we found you," said Keir. The woods where they had met had been a strange place that seemed apart from this world in a way that seemed alternately sinister and beautiful.

Genn laughed. "You humans always doubt our magic. But I didn't think you of all people would be one to doubt the power of the old ways. You who have seen them firsthand."

"It seems I have a lot of doubts lately."

"The wedding?"

"How did you—?" But Genn gave him a look like, *what did I just say?* And Keir stopped himself. "Yes, the wedding."

Genn flitted to take a seat in the horse's mane. The horse stirred but did not startle, another effect of the fairy's magic, perhaps.

"How could you doubt the one that led you from the dark corners of your own mind?"

"I don't doubt Alison. I doubt myself."

Genn nodded sagely. "Fair. But rather than doubt yourself, perhaps you should just try harder. If you're worried about failing to do something, perhaps just do it. If you're worried about doing something you shouldn't, perhaps don't."

Keir considered whether to brush the fairy off his horse and ride on. "Great advice. Why didn't I think of that?"

Genn laughed. "You misunderstand me. I'm not telling you to leave Alison or that she would be better off without you. I'm telling you that I think you are fully capable of being who she needs you to be. Love is a choice you make. Choose her, each and every day, but don't forget yourself. Find the balance. Sometimes it will be easy. Sometimes it will be hard. If I thought you were incapable, I would tell you so."

Keir couldn't decide whether to be comforted by the words or disturbed by how much the fairies seemed to know of him and Alison despite only having met once before. But heeding the fairy's advice, for Alison's sake, he chose comfort. "Thank you. I'll think on what you've said."

"Oh, and if you've ever gone and made a right mess of it, ask her to dance. There's no way she could stay angry with you long if you're dancing."

The fairy stood and stretched its back and wings, then flitted away, following the fairy fire into the woods on the other side of the road.

"Will you come to the wedding?" asked Keir just before they left sight. "Alison would want me to ask, at least."

"Of course," said Genn as the fairy fire flickered, vanishing from sight.

⁓⊙⊙⊙⁓

"No, no, no," said Willow. "Try again."

"Willow, I'm not a writer. I'm not even much of a talker. I don't know how I'm meant to do this."

Keir sat at his desk surrounded by crumpled up pieces of paper and scratched out lines. He'd been at it since the cat had woken him at midday with news of Alison's finalized vows.

Vows that she had apparently written herself.

"She wanted it to be a surprise, but I thought you'd be embarrassed if you showed up empty handed. Since I've heard hers, I can listen to yours and let you know if they work together."

Which was thoughtful of the cat—she was right that Keir would have been embarrassed to have to read the standard vows after Alison had poured her heart out—but Alison was a poet. Words were her gift.

Keir wasn't even great at saying comforting things to his patients. In fact, on more than one occasion since their return, he'd wished she could join him again on his house calls, and not just for the pain relief her magic was able to provide.

But he didn't want to keep her from the wedding planning or to monopolize the last of her time as a single woman, and so he'd made do with his own inadequate faculties.

Those same faculties were proving equally inadequate in describing his feelings for her.

"I promise to love you in good times and bad—"

"See, that's what I'm saying. Do you really want to focus on bad times at the wedding?"

"But that's traditional. The standard vows have a similar bit."

"So it's not very original, is it?"

Keir sighed. "Just give me a hint about what she's written."

"Try to be more specific," said Willow. "Less platitudes, more details. Let the audience fill in the generalities."

Well, Keir had to hand it to the cat. That was actually useful advice. Alison had mentioned that Willow made a fine editor, but Keir had thought she was just being kind.

It took the rest of the afternoon, but he finally came up with something decent. It wouldn't win any awards, but it was heartfelt and heavy on the specifics Willow had mentioned.

"You'll keep it a secret, won't you? I'd like it to be a surprise to her on the day."

Willow purred in response.

"And you too, Dinah?" asked Keir. The caramel cat was curled up on the couch. She'd been sleeping for most of the day, but Keir couldn't be sure what she had heard.

"Food," said Dinah.

"Too right," said Keir, heading into the kitchen.

⚬⟨◎⟩⚬

Back at New Year's, Keir had spent some time looking through boxed up things in the cellar of Weldan House while Alison had gotten dressed for the ball.

It hadn't taken him long to find what he was looking for.

There were only a few pictures of Keir's mother that had been taken with a picture-taker. A traveling dwarf had visited Fossholm one Winter Solstice before Charlotte was born. He had come up to Weldan House with his picture-taker and a number of other strange contraptions, and Keir's father had turned him away.

But hearing of the picture-taker, Keir's mother had chased after the man, running down the gravel drive still in her slippers and dressing gown. She'd insisted he stay for Solstice supper that evening after taking their portraits in the afternoon. The dwarf had obliged, and Lady Ainsley had been most generous in her praise and compensation. Lord Ainsley, despite his earlier misgivings, had gone along with the affair willingly.

She had been the one person he couldn't say no to.

The portraits themselves were boxed away with Lady Ainsley's other things after her passing. Keir didn't remember the day himself, but he'd heard the story from the servants, and he'd gone looking for the portraits. He went back every time he forgot his mother's face, which happened unfortunately often. How cruel memory could be, to give access to some terrible things so easily while denying him the beautiful moments he most longed for.

At least this one moment had been preserved. Keir hadn't seen the portraits since the beginning of the latest feud with his father, having been unwelcome from Weldan House for all those years. Seeing her face again after relying for so long on his imperfect recollection was deeply gratifying. It soothed some aching part of him he had forgotten existed but that was always there, gnawing at his peace.

Keir wondered as he carried the portrait of his mother alone—the smallest of the prints, one made to fit exactly into the kind of locket he'd given Alison— whether Alison felt the same way thinking of her father. She had known him much longer than Keir had known his mother, and her feelings regarding him must have been more complex than the simple longing he'd felt for a woman whose absence had shaped his entire life. Did she forget his face in the same way?

Could she remember his voice?

Keir would have given anything to remember his mother's voice. But he also wondered that if he did, if he remembered more of her in his own memories apart from the ones the servants had shared with him, if it would have been harder on him when he thought of her. If knowing her more would have given him more to miss.

He knocked on the cottage door; an unnecessary formality, he knew, but it didn't feel right to intrude on Alison's private space unannounced. She had shed her flannel nightgown in favor of the pretty slip with yellowing lace she often wore beneath it, and Keir could see why: it was quite warm in the cottage with the fire going now that they'd repaired all of the cracks and gaps in the floors and walls.

"Charlotte stopped by and told me you were back late, but the baby came alright," said Alison as she took his cloak. It was the same cloak he'd given her the first time they'd met, a night not much warmer than this one nearly a year earlier.

It had been such a shock seeing her there in his stream. Her stream, really, she had been right about that. She'd been so small and pale in the moonlight when she'd taken the cloak, shivering. So fragile.

Of course, he'd later learned she wasn't very fragile at all, but the moment had awoken something else in him he'd kept buried: the need to care for someone.

She had needed him so rarely since then. Would she ever need him like that again?

"Is that the portrait?" asked Alison, spotting the envelope in his hand. "May I see it?"

Keir nodded, handing it to her wordlessly.

"Oh," said Alison. "She was blonde! I had always pictured her with darker hair like yours or mine. You know, I always thought you and Charlotte resembled your father, but now that I'm looking at her, I can really see her in—"

"Charlotte, I know," said Keir. "I had forgotten too."

Of course, his memories of Charlotte ended so abruptly and with such a different version of her. He felt a pang of regret to have not known a younger Charlotte.

"She was so beautiful. And such a lovely smile. It was rare back then to take a smiling portrait like this. You're lucky to have it."

"Do you remember your father's smile?"

Alison took the portrait of his mother and put it with the locket. Then she led him to the couch to sit together in front of the fire. "I do," she said, smiling herself. Keir wondered how much of her smile was shared with her father. "He had a little gap between his front teeth. It was barely noticeable, but he liked to whistle through it to make me laugh."

She turned to Keir, a serious look in her big blue eyes. "Are you certain about not having your father at the wedding? I know it's complicated, but when he finds out—"

"I don't care what he thinks when he finds out. I'm certain." Keir had given a lot of thought to whether or not to attempt reconciliation. The last time he'd seen Lord Ainsley, he had punched him in the nose. He hadn't regretted it—it was long overdue, if anything—but he imagined it would make achieving anything beyond the peace they'd struck then, a peace built entirely on Keir's demands which Lord Ainsley had been too shocked to deny, difficult. To say the least.

"There's also the matter of Charlotte," he said. "She doesn't wish for him to know she's alive, which I've told her is something we won't be able to keep secret forever, but there wouldn't be any denying who she was if she showed up at the wedding."

"No, certainly not," said Alison, glancing at the portrait on the desk. The family resemblance was unmistakable.

"And if I have to choose who I'd rather have at my wedding, it would be my sister every single time."

"Of course," said Alison. "It's a shame about your father, but I understand."

"Your mother's still coming though?"

Alison laughed. "As if Violet Lennox would ever miss her only daughter's wedding," she said, putting on a voice with a high degree of enunciation that Keir imagined he'd be hearing much more of soon. "She arrives the week before. And hopefully leaves directly after. I love her, but there's only so much of her I can take."

Alison shifted back to look at Keir more directly. "There was another thing I wanted to discuss. The vicar—"

"—is horrible," said Keir.

"No, not horrible!" said Alison, laughing. "He's just—"

"Old-fashioned, judgmental, impersonal, aggressively unpleasant to be around, and a bore."

"Keir!"

Keir usually reserved his vitriol for his father, but he had overheard the vicar speaking about "preserving the natural order" and "not defying the vision of the Gods" recently, and it had rubbed him the wrong way.

Alison, who had not grown up around here, had been willing to give the vicar the benefit of the doubt, but now that she was seeing him for who he was, Keir felt he could no longer hold his tongue. "I'm sorry, darling, but I'd really rather he didn't marry us."

"That's what I was thinking too," admitted Alison. "But who else could do it? The wedding is in less than a month."

Keir groaned. "There's always Idris," he said. Truthfully, he wasn't concerned about Idris grandstanding or taking away attention from them. In fact, he wouldn't mind it much if he did. "But in case you haven't noticed, I don't have a surplus of friends around here. You have your maid of honor. I'd feel odd without a best man."

"Do you know any judges? Any of the nobility who wouldn't mind?"

Keir's father could do it, he supposed, although he was certainly the last person they would ask.

"We could have an anvil wedding," Keir realized.

"A what?"

"An anvil wedding. Some couples from Loegria come up here when their families don't approve of their marriage. Anyone who owns property can technically marry a couple here, as long as there's a witness and the banns have been read. It's often the blacksmith that does it. We're pretty far from the sea here, but Weyland may have even done it before."

Alison's eyes lit up at the mention of Weyland. "Really? Why didn't you mention it earlier?"

"It's not viewed as particularly honorable. I didn't want to shame you." Keir felt as though it was shameful enough marrying in secret without his father knowing. "I didn't want to rob you of the traditional wedding experience if that was what you wanted."

Alison laughed. "I don't care about tradition. I don't care about any of it really. I just want to marry you. Let's have an anvil wedding. If Weyland is too shy to do it, I'm sure Gwenla wouldn't mind. She's a property owner."

She kissed him on the cheek, and it soothed any worry he had felt. He *could* make her happy. Maybe Genn was right. Maybe it wouldn't always be easy, but maybe all he needed to do was keep trying. "An anvil wedding, then. But perhaps at the town hall rather than the forge. I don't think everyone we've invited will fit."

"Perfect," said Alison, this time kissing him on the lips. Gods, she was so soft and lovely. This beautiful, perfect woman who would be his wife. "You know," she said, her voice dropped low, "there are other things I'm not traditional about."

"I know that, and I love it," said Keir, slipping the lace from her shoulder.

Chapter Fifteen

FURTHER PREPARATIONS

Alison

Later in the week, Alison had her dress fitting at Lydiach's shop.

She was still feeling a bit embarrassed about her first visit. Now that Rinka had been in town for a while, the wedding planning was much more under control, and she no longer felt the overwhelming sense of too many choices she'd felt during the first consultation.

"Now, Alison. If you're unhappy with the design, there's still enough time to make another, though it will be tight. We can change the sleeves or the lace; I can bring up the hem. Don't be afraid to ask for what you like."

Alison didn't know much about what she liked, but she did know she liked the dress.

Rinka explained it to her as Lydiach placed pins in a few places, marking where to make adjustments. "You wanted something organic, so we went with this floral lace. See how it follows the lines of the dress like it's growing from the ground beneath your feet? And we did sheer layers of the chiffon you liked draped into the train. Nothing too long or showy, just enough to blend it all together. And the sleeves—"

Alison let out a sob as Lydiach placed a matching chiffon veil on her head and a delicate wool shawl on her shoulders.

"Oh, are you alright?" asked Lydiach.

"Did I go too fast?" asked Rinka. "Sorry, I got a bit excited—"

"No, no," said Alison as Lydiach flew over a handkerchief. She lifted the veil, watching her reflection smile through her tears in the looking glass. "It's just so beautiful. I feel beautiful. It's exactly right."

"Oh, good!" said Lydiach. "Those are the tears we like to see."

Rinka nodded. "I felt that way the first time I put on one of Lydiach's dresses. She's a miracle worker."

"Nonsense," said Lydiach. "I just highlight what's already there."

"This will be you soon enough," said Alison to Rinka as she changed back into her plain blue dress. It looked strange on her now, like the wedding dress had revealed who she really was, and these clothes belonged to a stranger.

"I heard about that. Congratulations!" said Lydiach on the other side of the screen. "A royal wedding. When's the big day?"

"A long way off," said Rinka. "There's going to be another interview with the same magazine to announce it in a few weeks. It'll take most of the year to plan. Idris wants to have it here in Wilderise, but we'll see what the king says. Queen Yuling may even attend."

Rinka had told Alison the truth about Queen Yuling's separation from the king. They had sent her a copy of their magazine debut and had just recently received a lovely letter of congratulations from her delivered all the way to Weldan House from Formosa. Alison imagined it must have been hard for her to be so distant from her children, and she was glad to hear that she might come to the wedding even though that might be difficult for her, too.

"A royal wedding in Wilderise! I hope you'll think of me, not for the wedding dress, per se, but if you needed any other gowns—"

"Lydiach, I would not have anyone else dress me. Let's get Alison married first, then we can all come look at designs. Idris tells me that the traditional Formosan gowns are lovely and would suit my red hair, at least for one of the events… "

Alison was glad it was Rinka and not her that would be dealing with all the pageantry of a royal wedding. Her simple village affair was more than enough.

"Don't lose any more weight before the wedding," said Lydiach as they were on their way out. Alison had been neglecting her diet a bit lately. She forgot to eat sometimes when she was focused on her poetry.

"Let's pop in and see Charlotte and Mrs. Knox next door," said Rinka. "They'll fill you out nicely with those biscuits of theirs."

They thanked Lydiach and headed over to the bakery. They had originally planned on getting some of the delicious chocolate biscuits with the swirly tops to go with their tea, but Charlotte had just finished making some new truffle varieties and wanted their opinion before putting them on sale.

"This one has a hazelnut in the middle. I can't decide if I like it better with the nut for the crunch, or if I like this one where we ground them into a cream."

"Crunch, definitely," said Alison as Mrs. Knox poured the tea and joined them at the table.

"Charlotte, bring them out some of the heart-shaped biscuits too."

"Coming right up."

"Did you hear those constables are back in town?" asked Mrs. Knox.

"DCI Tirrin and DC Lord Wexenas?" asked Alison.

Mrs. Knox raised her eyebrows. "Did you meet them last year? During the ink theft debacle?"

The accidental theft had happened just down the street at Mezec's shop when Strelka had been trying to secure inks for Weyland. Alison herself had been a prime suspect in the crime, having only just arrived in town. "They questioned me," she said. The questioning had been a farce, but they had done it, nonetheless. "What's happened now?"

"I heard it from Mr. Rainey that they're after that thatcher from Fossholm, Mr. Craig. They say he scammed someone in Fossholm out of their coin, and he's on the run," said Charlotte as she brought over the heart-shaped biscuits.

"These are really pretty," said Rinka, admiring the frosting on a biscuit a moment before stuffing the entire thing into her mouth. "Taste good too," she said before tearing into the next one.

"Did you say Mr. Craig?" asked Alison. "He tried to rip me off in the spring when my roof was leaking. Keir had to talk him down."

"You should tell the detectives that," said Mrs. Knox. "They're staying at the inn."

"Did you hear that Mezec is bringing one of the korrigans to your wedding?" asked Charlotte.

Alison sat back, sipped her tea, and nibbled on the wonderful biscuits Mrs. Knox and Charlotte had made while she listened to all of the gossip, grateful for a day of girly chat.

Afterwards, they headed down to the forge to see Weyland. She had three purposes to her visit: to collect Keir's ring, to drop of her updated manuscript so Weyland could finish the illustrations, and to ask him for the small favor of officiating her wedding.

Weyland was happy to give her the ring—it was just what she asked for—and thrilled to work on the manuscript again.

"This is a new one," he said, holding up the last poem Alison had added. It was a bit of a different style from the others.

The world is never more silent
Than it is in winter.
The dizzying traffic of everyday
Slowed to almost nothing.
A flit of wings. A snap of branch.

Time stands still.
Only thoughts remain.
Dreaming of spring,
Arms outstretched,
Yearning for rebirth.

But the ice grows in the cracks,
Filling them. Holding them.
Trapped at first, but slowly finding peace.
Acceptance.

Lost in the frozen moment,
Listening.
A pair of footsteps, soft,
Are moving closer.

A light shines through glittering branches.
They drip and bend,
But do not break.

"This is my favorite of all of them," said Weyland when he finished reading. "I hope I can capture it."

Alison was certain that he would. But as enthusiastic as Weyland was about the poetry book, he was much more skeptical about officiating the wedding.

"Do I really seem like the right sort for that?" he asked. "You can have the anvil. I'll even take it to the town hall for you."

"You wouldn't have to do much. I'm writing my vows, so you'd just need to read the standard ones for Keir…"

Alison looked into her friend's face as he grew even more red than usual. On the one hand, he didn't want to tell her no. But on the other hand, he really, really wanted to tell her no.

"Never mind, Weyland. You've done enough for us. I do think the anvil would be fun to have though."

That meant she'd need to find Gwenla to ask her. It was mid-afternoon; maybe she'd run into her collecting Finnli from the schoolhouse on the way back.

She parted ways with Rinka, who was due in Fossholm for some sort of meeting regarding their college construction plans. But before she could find Gwenla, she ran into someone else: DC Lord Wexenas.

"Hello, detective. I hear you're looking for Mr. Craig."

DC Lord Wexenas looked around him as if he hadn't noticed Alison coming despite his keen elvish senses. "Ah, I remember you. Ink theft, wasn't it? Are you in cahoots with Craig?"

"What?" Alison regarded the young elf. He'd pulled his golden hair back into a more sensible bun, and he had a small scar on his forehead, but he otherwise seemed as much of a fool as he had been last spring. "The ink wasn't even stolen, remember? And no, I haven't seen Mr. Craig since he tried to overcharge me for my roof repair."

"Just what someone harboring a fugitive might say—"

"Forgive my colleague here," said DCI Tirrin. The old dwarf constable seemed even more exasperated than the last time Alison had seen him. "He's been stuck behind a desk most of the year. What did you say about Mr. Craig overcharging?"

Alison filled the detectives in on what she knew of Mr. Craig, ignoring DC Lord Wexenas's obvious skepticism and her own questions about what he'd done to earn so much desk work.

"As a local, do you have any ideas about where he'd hide?" asked DCI Tirrin.

A local. No one had called Alison that before. And it wasn't even coming from the delusional Lord Wexenas.

"There aren't many good hiding places in winter. The stables near the inn, maybe, or the dwarven mine up the mountain, if he could convince them to have him."

"Thank you," said DCI Tirrin. "By the way, are you the one marrying Dr. Ainsley?"

"You mean this is the future marchioness?" asked DC Lord Wexenas, his mouth hanging open in disbelief.

"I am," said Alison. She drew herself up into her most future-Marchioness-of-Caernock stance. It may not have been impressive in height, but she hoped it seemed exceptionally smug.

"Oh, forgive me, my lady," said Lord Wexenas. "I knew not of whom I was speaking with."

"That much was obvious," said Alison.

Lord Wexenas was really getting fired up now. "My lady, we'll do everything in our power to keep you safe from brigands and scoundrels and—"

"Yes, yes, I think she understands," said DCI Tirrin. "Good day, ma'am. And blessings upon your marriage."

Alison thanked the constables and set off once more to find Gwenla, dodging the 'lectric installers who had made it to the streetlamps on the Herot's Hollow High Street.

Gwenla wasn't in any of the shops or at the schoolhouse, or at the inn or the post office. Alison finally found her outside her cottage tending the garden.

"See here?" asked Gwenla, pointing to thin green stems rising out of the earth in clumps. "Know what they are?"

"Daffodils," said Alison. "Is it really time again?" They had been blooming when Alison first arrived.

"They've got a ways to go before they flower, but spring will be here soon enough. I spotted some snowdrops in the churchyard. It'll be lovely by the time the wedding comes."

"I actually wanted to speak with you about that," said Alison. "We've decided not to be married in the church, or rather not to be married by the vicar—"

"What's old Lewis gone and done now? That miserable old git. Did he say something rude to you? Were you thinking of going with the vicar in Fossholm instead? It's a nice church as well, not as old as this one, but nice. Of course, we'll need to move the catering for the banquet. And the cake delivery. Did you speak with Rinka already?"

Alison hadn't realized Gwenla had been so intimately involved in the wedding planning, although she wasn't exactly surprised. "No, we're not thinking Fossholm. Keir says we can have an anvil wedding at the town hall."

"An anvil wedding! Don't tell me Weyland—now, you know I love him—"

"Weyland was…reluctant, but he did say he'd bring the anvil."

Gwenla laughed. "I didn't think you'd want the anvil without the blacksmith, but it is quite fun to hear it *plink* when the hammer strikes it. It reminds me of a dwarf wedding, though it's been a long time since I've been to one of those. So who's going to do the honors? Idris?"

Alison held her breath. "We were thinking you might do it."

"Me?" Gwenla was shocked. She put down her spade and dusted the dirt from her gloves onto her apron. "You do realize who you're asking. I'm not a vicar, or a judge, or a noble, or even a blacksmith."

"But you're a landowner, which means you can legally marry us here in Wilderise."

Gwenla lifted her head, considering that. "Well, Lady Willana did leave me the property. A shame she's not still with us. She would've been the perfect officiant."

"Maybe you could think of what she'd say," said Alison. She knew the dwarf often thought of Lady Willana's perspective.

"She would have loved to see me try. She knew I'm not much of a speaker, but she liked to listen to me anyway."

Alison didn't agree that Gwenla wasn't much of a speaker. She'd heard a number of her speeches, and she thought she was terrific: a bit frank, maybe, but genuine and relatable.

"So you'll consider it at least?"

"Oh, alright," said Gwenla. "If it's what you both want, how can I say no? I just hope you won't be disappointed with me if I say the wrong thing. I might go and pronounce you married to the wrong man."

"I'm sure you won't," said Alison, laughing. "Thank you, Gwenla. You know, you helped me a lot back when things were difficult with Keir in the beginning. Without you, we might not be here." She gave the dwarf a hug over her protests about the dirt on her apron.

"I'm just so glad you came. I didn't think I'd have much of a life after Lady Willana left. It turns out, there was a lot more left for me to do."

"And there still is," said Alison.

Gwenla smiled. "Starting with learning what happens at a human wedding."

Chapter Sixteen

A CHANGE OF PLANS

Charlotte

Charlotte had seen little of Julian since their fight. His delivery must have arrived as scheduled because the queue outside his shop had returned, but Charlotte could see little point in asking him about it. He'd made his position clear enough the last time they spoke. He still hadn't answered their window display challenge, but he had taken so much of their sandwich trade that Mrs. Knox had considered giving it up altogether in favor of sweets.

So when she spotted him on her way to the inn after a visit with the korrigans (in which she caught up on all the latest gossip regarding the korrigan Senara and her new beau Mezec, the fairy apothecary of Herot's Hollow), she wasn't sure whether to say anything.

She settled for watching him from a distance. He was out in front of his shop, unloading something heavy from a cart with the help of the hobgoblins Marty and Gary from down at the inn. He'd gotten help from the right people; they were strong despite their diminutive size.

Of course, since it was Julian, he hadn't asked them for help at all—he'd hired them, as Charlotte saw when he paid them. And Marty and Gary, like Mr. Rainey, would not refuse payment if offered, even though they gladly would have done the task for free.

Perhaps Charlotte ought to look in his shop for the swindler Mr. Craig. If anyone around here was likely to get taken for a ride, it was Julian.

Marty and Gary waved to Charlotte as they brought the cart back to the inn. They had unfortunate tim-ing—Julian had just returned from inside the store to pick up a paper he'd dropped, and he spotted her lurk-ing in the shadows.

Charlotte turned and headed towards Orchard Lane.

"Charlotte, wait," he called after her.

She stopped, trying to decide whether to turn around. He jogged down the cobblestone street be-hind her, then came around her to face her when she refused to look at him.

"That stove I ordered, it's 'lectric," he said. "I had one back in the city. They can bake a bit unevenly, but it's easier to control the heat in them. Perfect for tricky things like cheesecakes."

What was the point of telling her that? "That's nice," she said, although her face said quite the opposite.

Julian stiffened. "I thought I'd give you fair warning. Now that the 'lectrics are being installed, I'm sure you'll be doing the same soon enough."

"We will," said Charlotte, although she didn't actually know if Mrs. Knox had ordered a stove or planned to do so anytime soon. The 'lectrics hadn't been installed yet on their side of the street.

"Good," said Julian.

"Is that all?" It definitely was not all Charlotte wanted to say, so she doubted it was all Julian wanted to say. Standing here in the street with him, she could so easily forget the decades that had come between them. She wanted to ask him if he would race her to the inn, if he would come with her to the stone circle by Alison's cottage to watch for falling stars, if he would help her play a prank on Keir.

But even if time apart had meant nothing, this rivalry wasn't so easily put aside, especially when it seemed nothing had changed. He would not bend.

He had said nothing, but Charlotte was sick of waiting. She sighed and moved past him.

"Wait," said Julian, grabbing her arm.

The gesture wasn't forceful, but it shocked Charlotte. "What are you doing?"

"Sorry," said Julian, quickly letting her go. "Sorry, that was too familiar. For a minute, I felt like we were children again. I'm sorry. I know we aren't."

Charlotte looked at the ground, trying not to think of the thrill that went through her at his touch. "What did you want to say?"

"I don't know," said Julian, holding his head in his hand and looking up at the sky. "I just. Gods, I don't know, Charlotte. I don't want it to be like this."

"It doesn't have to be!" said Charlotte. "You're making a choice. You could choose to trust me instead. We could help you. We could work together—"

"I can't. I want to believe you, but I have too much to lose. I worked so hard to build this for myself. I can't let it go, not without—"

"I'm not asking you to let it go. We could work something out. Make a list of what you bake and what we bake. Or a schedule. Something to stop this pointless competition. Don't you see how that would be better for you too? It's not a zero-sum game. If we win, you don't have to lose. We can both win." Charlotte sighed again; she couldn't let it go unsaid any longer.

"I don't want to be your enemy. Julian, I...I missed you."

Julian leaned forward suddenly and pulled her to him, kissing her on the lips.

Before she could even react, he pulled away. "Gods, I'm sorry. I don't know what I'm doing. I'm sorry, I'm sorry."

This time, it was Charlotte who called for him as he hurried away. "Wait!"

But Julian kept going, leaving Charlotte standing there alone.

Gods, what the hells was *that*?

⚜

It was difficult to focus on her work at the bakery after what had happened with Julian, but it wasn't a good week to be distracted: it was the week of Keir and Alison's wedding.

Charlotte made a note to berate Keir for his decision to get married during the celebration of Lupercalia, the busiest time of the year for the bakery apart from Winter Solstice. She and Mrs. Knox had been working around the clock to put together boxes of truffles and macarons and other sweet treats for the villagers, leaving them little time to practice and perfect the wedding cakes.

But the worst was yet to come.

"Mrs. Knox. Mrs. Knox!" Someone was banging on the door to the bakery more than an hour before opening.

Mrs. Knox was up to her elbows in bread dough, leaving Charlotte to see what was going on.

It was the postman. "Urgent pigeon arrived for Mrs. Moira Knox," he said, placed a letter in her hand. "Will you see that she gets it?"

"Of course," said Charlotte.

Charlotte carried the letter to the back, regarding it nervously.

"Is that a blue envelope?" asked Mrs. Knox. The blue envelopes of urgent deliveries were expensive and rarely held good news. "Can you read it to me?"

Charlotte hoped this would be one of the rare blue letters with a happy surprise in it as she tore it open.

Moira,

I hate to trouble you like this after so long, but I've had a bit of a fall.

"Who is it from?"

Charlotte flipped the letter over. "Martha?"

"My sister."

The doctor said my hip will heal, but I'm meant to keep off my feet for a time, and I don't have anyone around who can help. But first, I have to get through the operation on Saturday. They said it would be good if I could have someone who can help me home, and I'm afraid with Arthur gone, I didn't know who else to ask.

I know it's an imposition to ask you to come all this way and on such short notice. But the operation itself is costing me dearly, and I just can't afford the kind of care they say I'll need with what's left of Arthur's coin.

I hope you're well and that the new apprentice is ready to take on a bit more for a short time. Do let me know if you're coming.

All my love,
Martha

Mrs. Knox stopped kneading the dough and looked up. "It's been twenty years since I've seen her. I never left, but she used to come here." She scraped the dough off her hands and from between her fingers. "Charlotte, I know I'm asking a lot of you, but you can do this. I wrote all the instructions down. There are timings for everything. Add a couple of hours to the prep and decorating time since you'll be on your own."

"You're leaving right now?" asked Charlotte. She had known when she read the letter that Mrs. Knox would go, but she thought she'd wait until after the wedding cakes were baked.

"Martha lives in Arcas Dyrne. If I borrow a horse from Mr. Rainey and leave now, I still may not make it in time for her operation. I'm so sorry to do this to you, but it's why you're here. I know you can do it, Charlotte."

Charlotte looked out over the countless containers of ingredients and the empty pans. She knew the steps. She'd practiced the techniques. But the wedding cakes were going to be huge. All that piping, and nowhere to hide her mistakes…

"Don't worry about Lupercalia. We should have enough chocolates to get us through. And if the bread doesn't get baked tomorrow, well, Julian has his shop. I never thought I'd be happy for that, but here we are. No one in this town is going hungry, that's for sure."

Mrs. Knox was taking off her apron. She really was leaving, and Charlotte was really going to do this on her own.

"I'm heading up to pack and get changed. Breathe, Charlotte. Take it one step at a time."

"Take care," said Charlotte, coming out of her daze. "I hope Martha's operation goes well."

Mrs. Knox grinned. "She's a tough old thing. I know it must have killed her to have sent the letter. In truth, I'll be glad to see her again. Twenty years is far too long."

It was. Charlotte knew that firsthand.

Charlotte read through Mrs. Knox's notes while she packed upstairs, grateful that she was so detailed in her instructions. Maybe she could do this. She'd made plenty of cakes, and she'd been practicing the decorations for weeks. And Keir and Alison were unlikely to be critical, although she still didn't want to disappoint them. Not after everything they'd done for her.

The plan was fairly simple: today, she would make the cake batters, fillings, and sugar flower decorations. Tomorrow, she'd bake the cakes, cool them, and then do most of the assembly. Then Saturday, the morning of the wedding, she would finish the piping and decorations. She crossed out the timings on Mrs. Knox's plans and added extra hours to anything that might require more attention or that may need to be redone. It added up to a late night or two with her additions, but there was enough time if she was careful and meticulous in her execution.

Before Mrs. Knox left, she quickly sketched the designs she'd been planning. "Be careful on the placement of the flowers. Don't get too cute with it.

Allow for some asymmetry; it gives it the more natural feeling Alison prefers."

"I'll do my best," said Charlotte.

"I know you will," said Mrs. Knox, and she was on her way.

Alone, Charlotte got to work. She finished up her daily tasks without much incident, finishing the bread Mrs. Knox was baking and the croissants they had prepared the night before. She even had time to make a batch of the chili-spiced truffles she'd added to their Lupercalia menu before getting started on the wedding cakes.

The sponges themselves were simple: Alison and Keir had chosen ordinary vanilla and chocolate, and all she had to do today was mix together the batters. They'd chill overnight in the icebox, which Mrs. Knox said was both good for saving time tomorrow and for developing the flavors. The mixing was tiring work for as many bowls of batter as she needed to make—each cake would have four layers and two tiers for a total of eight cake pans per cake, which was an awful lot of cake. Charlotte idly wondered if Julian had ordered a 'lectric mixer to go with his 'lectric stove; it would have spared her arms a lot of trouble.

But she was too afraid to face him. She wasn't sure which she dreaded more: that he might tell her it was a terrible mistake, and he never should have kissed her;

or that he might tell her that it wasn't, and he was glad he did.

She had felt those confusing feelings under the mistletoe weeks earlier in spite of their rivalry, and she had felt even more confusing feelings since the kiss. There was still something of the bond they'd shared in childhood there, that was certain, and there was something so familiar and comforting about being around him, something that made her feel like she didn't have to pretend in his presence, that she could be exactly who she was.

That was when he wasn't being an arse about the bakery, at least.

Charlotte finally finished all the batter, filling most of their large icebox with bowl after bowl. Next up was the fillings. Champagne and chocolate Gallic meringues, strawberry and raspberry jams, and white chocolate and plain chocolate ganaches to go on top. It was a pity Alison had hated the fondant so much—it was so much easier of a topping to work with than the ganache, but the almond flavor could be polarizing, and it didn't go well with the fillings she'd chosen anyway.

The Gallic meringues came together quickly, although Charlotte's arms felt as though they might fall off by the time she was done whipping them, even with the help of the manual beaters. The jams had already been made, so it was just a matter of measuring out the quantity required. Mrs. Knox liked to have everything measured and prepared before beginning to bake, something she called *mise en place*, a Gallic convention that ensured that everything required was ready and available before the time-sensitive tasks began.

The two types of chocolate ganache were where the trouble began. The truffles she'd made just that morning used nearly the same recipe, and so she'd been overly confident in her abilities. Her first attempt came out grainy—she'd been impatient and had begun whisking the chocolate and cream together too soon.

No matter. She tried again, but this time she scorched the cream while trying to multi-task and chop chocolate at the same time. She swore—a lot—as she dumped the cream into a waste bucket and threw the pan into the wash basin. It was a problem for future Charlotte.

Her third attempt was interrupted by a knock at the door. "We're closed," she called, not wanting to pause the heating process.

"Charlotte, it's Gwenla. Open up!"

Charlotte sighed as she removed the cream from the heat. It would probably still work when she resumed, but baking could be so finicky that there was always the chance that starting and stopping could ruin some-thing entirely.

"What's going on?" she asked Gwenla as she let her inside.

"Did you feel that breeze just now? The tempera-ture's dropping fast out there. It looks like a storm's coming. I'm going around to make sure everyone has plenty of firewood and supplies."

Charlotte leaned out the door to see for herself. There was quite a chill compared to when she'd arrived in the morning, and the sky had gone completely grey. "What about the wedding? Keir and Alison's guests are meant to arrive tonight and tomorrow."

"I know," said Gwenla. "I sent a pigeon to Fossholm to see if any of the folks staying there can come up to-day. With any luck, it'll just settle up in the mountains and miss us entirely. But be ready, just in case."

Charlotte thanked Gwenla and resumed the ga-nache making, this time with a bit more urgency. She knew they were low on firewood at Keir's house, and she doubted he'd be home in time to take care of it.

Unfortunately, urgency and baking did not mix. This time, the cream was too hot, and the chocolate separated.

"Argh! I've done this a hundred times. Why can't I do it when it counts?" Charlotte shouted into the empty bakery.

There was something that might help though. Something sitting in a shop across the street that offered far better temperature control than the wood stove she was working on.

She didn't need Julian's help, and she certainly wouldn't ask for it under normal circumstances. But being able to use his stove would cut down on the time the rest of the tasks would take dramatically, assuming it meant she could get them right on the first try.

It was for this reason that she crossed the street to his shop. There were no ulterior motives, no secret desires that were threatening to come to the surface. Nothing but pure practicality.

It had begun to snow by the time Charlotte walked into the street for the second time, and the wind was blowing so hard Charlotte barely heard Gwenla shouting at her.

"Charlotte! He's gone. Julian's gone."

She handed Charlotte a hand-written note, the wind nearly whipping it out of her grip before she could read it.

Closed early for a delivery in the mountains. Back in the morning.

   -   *Mr. Julian Blair, Proprietor*

"The mountains?"

"Gods, he'll never make it back in this," said Gwenla. "The mountains always get it worse than here in town."

"I'll go," said Charlotte. "The korrigan magic—I can stand the cold better than most. I'll make sure he makes it back."

"Oh, bless you, girl," said Gwenla.

"Get home before you freeze to death. You've done what you can."

"Aye, I think you're right. Oh, I hope it melts off before the wedding! A white wedding is one thing, but this?"

It was far too much. Even Charlotte felt the chill down to her bones. The korrigans were tough, but they had their limits. There were few things that could survive in this kind of cold.

And humans were not one of them.

Charlotte ran up the High Street, past the forge, and up the path into the mountains. Julian hadn't said exactly where his delivery would take him, and any tracks he might have made had been covered by the newly fallen snow. But Charlotte had a guess—there was a dwarf who kept a cottage on the hillside near the lumber mill that supplied the mines, and he had a sweet tooth.

She made it to the turn off for the cottage, or where she thought the turn off was, at least. It was hard to tell in the blizzard. But she should have been able to see the smoke coming from the dwarf's chimney from here. Maybe the wind was too strong to see it.

Charlotte breathed heavily as she raced up the winding path. At least the exertion was warming her up a little, although the air felt like ice in her lungs. What if she was heading to the wrong house, and Julian was stuck somewhere else? By the time she found him, it might be too late.

Or he might not be in trouble at all. Perhaps he'd made it to the dwarf's house, and they were enjoying a cup of tea by the fire, waiting for it all to blow over.

Or maybe he had passed her somehow and had made it back to the bakery, and she was the only one who was in danger.

She could warm up by the dwarf's fire if nothing else. Then she could keep going, either to find Julian or to return home, once she caught her breath.

She had almost made it to the cottage's steps when she spotted something off the path half buried in the snow.

"Julian!"

Chapter Seventeen

A WINTERY ARRIVAL

Alison

The day before the wedding, Alison woke to find a foot of snow had fallen overnight.

She had received Gwenla's warning on the way back from dropping off her completed poetry book at the post office, and it had given her just enough time to find Keir at the inn (and to rescue him from her mother's endless questions) before the snow had started falling.

They had spent the evening in Alison's cottage—it was smaller and easier to keep warm. Alison hoped everyone else managed to keep warm as well, especially her out-of-town guests who were due to arrive today.

"Do you suppose they all made it to Fossholm last night before it started? Or do you think they turned back to Sudport when things got rough? I hope no one was trapped out there," said Alison as Keir dug out a path through the snow.

"I'm sure the carriages from Sudport knew what to do," said Keir. "Don't worry. Let's go down to the inn and greet them as they arrive."

"They're stuck on the road from Fossholm!" yelled Gwenla. The dwarf came tearing up the path from Orchard Lane, or where the path would have been if it hadn't been covered in snow. She had something strapped to her boots that resembled badminton rackets: snowshoes.

"Who's stuck?" asked Alison.

"Your aunt and cousin. Your mother wanted me to come get you. The driver rode into town to get help. Brytak has gone down there with his cart."

Aunt Rose and Eloise were city girls through and through. They were probably scared half to death stuck in an abandoned carriage. "Do you know if they're alright?" asked Alison.

"The carriage was closed, at least. They should manage for a couple of hours. I sent a pigeon to Sudport to see if Yordin and Marna have left yet. Oh, what a mess this is! At least the sun is out."

Rinka joined them then, likely having heard Gwenla's yelling all the way from Keir's house where she spent most nights. "Any sign of Idris yet? Or Ceri? Or Leo?"

"No," said Gwenla. "Although out of everyone, I'd worry about that lot the least."

Gwenla had a point. At least the royals had their magic to keep warm.

And so did Alison. "Come on," she said to Keir and Rinka. "We can fix this." She held out her hand and said out loud:

The situation is dire,
Let's have some fire.

Sparks flew from her hand onto the ground, instantly clearing a patch of snow and ice from the road.

"Where was that when I was shoveling our way out of the cottage?" said Keir.

"Sorry! I'm still not accustomed to having magic as an option."

"I'm only teasing. But next time, I'll let you handle it."

"Won't that wear you out?" asked Rinka. "There's a lot of snow on the road."

"That's what the two of you are for. Besides, we don't need to clear all of it. Just enough for the carriages to maneuver."

Alison set off down Orchard Lane, her Maid of Honor—a magical conduit—and her husband-to-be—a source of her magic—in tow.

"What about your mother?" called Gwenla after them. "What should I tell her?"

"Tell her we've gone to light the world on fire," said Alison, laughing.

⚜

They found Brytak and Alison's Aunt Rose and cousin Eloise about half an hour down the road to Fossholm.

Poor Brytak, the young orc whose family owned a farm near Herot's Hollow, was shoveling a path up an icy hill by hand while Rose and Eloise huddled together in the front of the cart, their cloaks wrapped around them for warmth.

Alison hadn't seen her aunt and cousin in a few years. Rose looked much the same as her mother—brown hair gone mostly grey, short statute, slim figure—but she had much finer clothes. Her husband was a solicitor, as she loved to remind them all every time they saw her.

Her cousin Eloise had barely been a teenager the last time Alison had seen her, but now she looked like a proper young woman. She was nearly as tall as her mother—at least she was sitting down—and her light brown hair, which she'd always worn in twin braids, was now in fashionable curls.

Alison was clearly not the only one who had noticed that Eloise was a proper young woman—Brytak was sneaking glances at her as he worked. And from the looks of it, Eloise was enjoying the attention.

"She's the right age for him," said Rinka quietly as they approached. "Oh, how cute that would be."

"Alison, Rinka, Dr. Ainsley," said Brytak. "What are you doing here?"

"We've come to rescue you," said Alison.

"With what?" asked Aunt Rose.

Alison hadn't thought of what she would tell her aunt. Surely even a solicitor's wife, a thoroughly modern woman, could see the utility in magic in an emergency.

"You'll see in a minute. Are you both alright?"

"We're fine," said Eloise. "Brytak has got us a lot further than the carriage driver did. He says we're almost there."

"Not long now," said Alison. "Thanks for the help, Brytak. Would you mind backing the cart up a bit?"

Brytak effortlessly pushed the cart back with his own muscle. Having heard just what Alison was capable of, he wisely backed out of the way himself.

Then Alison caught the road on fire.

"Oh, Gods! What are you doing?" cried Aunt Rose.

"Is that the old magic?" asked Eloise in an awed voice.

"It is," said Rinka. "Alison's quite a witch."

The fire didn't catch—the ground was much too wet for that. It simply melted the snow and ice in broad patches, some of it going up so quickly that it sublimated into a patch of fog.

It only took a few minutes to clear the hill. Alison felt the strain of the magic, but she still had a lot more in her. "Let's go," she said to Rinka and Keir. "It's clear the rest of the way into the town," she said to Brytak. "We're off to see if anyone else is in trouble."

"There's another carriage further in the woods," said Brytak. "I was going back for them after. Do you think you'll need me?" He was looking at Eloise as he spoke. Alison could guess how he'd rather spend his day.

"No, we'll manage," said Alison. "I'll see you at the inn later," she said to Aunt Rose and Eloise.

"Be careful!" said Aunt Rose. "Magic in this day and age. Not that I'm complaining. Thank you for the help, my dear!"

Alison and Rinka made a bet on whether Brytak would manage to get a dance from Eloise at the wedding against Keir. (They both thought he'd manage it, but Keir thought he would blow it before then.)

It took them longer than expected to reach the next stranded travelers. It was nearly an hour before they found Gwenla's cousin the industrialist dwarf Yordin, his wife Marna, and three of their children standing near a large carriage.

"Look, they've sent the bride and groom as a welcome party. And the future princess as well," said Yordin, shaking their hands. They didn't have to tell Yordin why they were there—Gwenla had let him know all about their magic when they were working on the power-savers that enabled the solar-generators to work even after the sun went down.

But their carriage driver was such a surprise, it took Alison a minute to recognize him. "Hyruk?"

The orc who drove the high-wheel carrier in Landsend had made it to Wilderise after all. "Hello, again," he said to Alison. "I see you made it to the ferry alright coming back."

"I did," said Alison. "I see you did as well. What happened to the high-wheel carrier?" The strange carriage that he pulled with a pedal-cycle was nowhere to be seen. The carriage he was driving Yordin's family in was pulled by horses.

"They're down in Sudport. I've got a few more of them now, but I got a carriage for longer rides in winter when business is slow. Although I heard a rumor they're building a manufactory up here. I might bring the high-wheelers up here. They're better in these hills. Although maybe what I ought to get is a sleigh for all this ice."

Alison cleared the large patch of it from the hillside as everyone looked on. This time, she drew on Keir and Rinka for support.

"Whoa!" said Hyruk, calming the horses as the first blast of fire hit the hill. Keir and Rinka's power was a lot for her to control—it was less like the delicate candle flames she made on her own and more like an explosion.

"I'll help you, darling," said Keir, taking her hand, his voice a little shaky.

"Sorry," said Alison. She hadn't meant to scare everyone. With Keir's help, the next blast was much more controlled. In no time at all, they had cleared the path.

"Did you pass anyone else?" asked Alison when they were done.

"No," said Hyruk. "We were the last ones leaving Fossholm. They were still waiting on the prince in Sudport when we left. I can't imagine they made it to Fossholm last night being that far behind us."

Rinka rubbed her gloved hands together nervously.

"I'm sure he's alright," said Alison. "Let's keep going to Fossholm. They're probably waiting in town for the roads to thaw."

The sun was nearly overhead by the time they'd reached Fossholm, and most of the ice was gone from the road even without Alison's fire. They'd passed more traffic—foot and horse—on the road, but no sign of Idris or any of the rest of the crew from Winwold.

"Over there!" someone yelled from the road that turned off to Weldan House. They looked where he was pointing; Rinka saw them first.

"It's Ceri!" she said. Alison and Keir couldn't see the white dragon against the blue sky at such a distance, but they believed her. "Oh Gods, she's carrying someone. And is that…?"

She burst into laughter. "Oh, he's going to be irate about this indignity."

"What is it?" asked Alison.

"You'll see in a minute."

Rinka waved her arms up at Ceri. Alison had no idea how Ceri could make her out from such a distance, but the dragon clearly was capable of it because she came in for a landing just a short time later.

As they grew closer, Alison saw what Rinka meant. Ceri was clutching Leo in her talons, and Idris was riding on her back.

And as they grew even closer, she could hear him shouting. "You're coming in too hot. Slow down. SLOW DOWN, YOU MANIAC!"

The "landing" was a bit more like a "crashing." Ceri's white wings tumbled into a shaded snowbank while the long limbs of her brother Idris and her partner Leo went flailing up around her.

"Are you alright?" said Keir, rushing over to help them. He pulled Idris to his feet while Ceri shifted back into her human form to help Leo.

"Sorry, darling," said the petite silver-haired princess as she picked him up off the ground. "I haven't landed with anyone in a while."

"I'm no worse for wear," said Leo, unbending his spectacles and removing the scarf that had been covering his face. The elf's cloak appeared ripped to Alison, but Leo quickly tucked it behind him to keep it from Ceri.

"I told you to slow down. You're lucky we weren't killed," said Idris.

"A dragon and an elf, killed by a bit of a rough landing? You do exaggerate," replied Ceri.

Keir looked like he wanted to say something regarding the tendency of all people to break under enough force, but he wisely kept his mouth shut. It was better to let Ceri and Idris squabble themselves out. Interfering could cause them to gang up against you.

"Did everyone else make it alright?" asked Ceri. "I've got to go back for Groundskeeper Tomasar and

Barney. The roads through the mountains outside of Sudport are impassable. It's still snowing back there."

Alison counted off the out-of-town guests on her hands. "I think that's everyone from Loegria once you bring Tomasar and Barney. Will they be okay to fly?"

"Tomasar is going to be terrified, but he's been terrified this entire trip. He'll manage with Barney there to comfort him," said Leo.

"Bless him," said Alison. "It was so good of him to come. I know he's really doing it for Willow."

"It's good for him to get out and see something other than that tree of his," said Leo. "I mean, it's a wonderful tree. Incredible magical properties. I've been measuring it quite a lot lately—"

"I'm heading out, darling," said Ceri, sparing the rest of them from one of Leo's lectures. *"Je t'adore."*

Idris mimed gagging gestures behind her back.

"Oh, stop," said Rinka. "You're worse than she is."

"And proud of it," said Idris, kissing Rinka for so long as to make everyone else uncomfortable. "I missed you."

"I missed you too," she said.

"And I missed you too," said Keir, making kissy noises at Idris. Alison loved to see them together. It brought out a playful side of Keir she rarely got to enjoy.

"Come on," said Idris. "Let's get back to town. We've got a wild night ahead of us."

"What do you mean?" asked Alison.

"It's your stag and hen nights!" said Rinka. "You didn't think we'd let you get married without a proper send off, did you?"

"Gods save us," said Keir.

❧❧❧

By the time they made it back to Herot's Hollow, Ceri had already arrived with Tomasar and Barney. The dog was playing chase with Willow and Dinah out in front of the inn, and the old dwarf was enjoying a pint at the bar with…Alison's mother?

"Mum?" asked Alison when she saw her. Could this really be her mother, drinking at a bar with a stranger?

"There you are," said Violet. Violet Lennox had a few more wrinkles around her green eyes than when Alison had seen her last, but she had also filled out a bit. She looked good, relaxed and comfortable in her skin. "They told me you were out there catching things on fire with magic. I know you weren't fond of number-crunching, but I hadn't realized you'd turn to pyromania."

Was that a joke? Was her mother actually joking?

Who was this woman, and what had she done with Violet Lennox?

"Your mother tells me she's due to retire from Gorluz Manufacturing," said Tomasar. "I was just telling her about Norgate."

"I'd like to see this yew of his. I told him I've never seen so many trees in my life as there are out here!"

"I'm glad you're having a good time, Mum. Did Auntie Rose and Eloise make it in alright?"

"Oh, yes. Rose is upstairs unpacking, and Eloise is going around town with an orc boy."

Brytak hadn't blown it yet, then. Keir was about to be out five gold.

Although come tomorrow, it would technically be both of their gold. So Alison and Keir would be out five gold to Rinka, she supposed.

Alison went around the inn, checking that everyone else was accounted for. She spotted Yordin and his family with Gwenla.

"Good job getting them all back here," said Gwenla. "Say, have you seen Charlotte come down the mountain yet?"

Oh, Gods. The mountains had gotten the worst of the storm. "Charlotte went up the mountain?"

Chapter Eighteen

THE CABIN IN THE MOUNTAINS

Charlotte

Charlotte flipped Julian's body over, brushing the snow off of him and trying to shake him awake.

"Julian! Julian, wake up. Julian!"

His skin was cold to the touch, but his body was warm, and at least he'd had the sense to bundle up and to cover his face with his scarf.

She pulled it back to check if he was still breathing.

"Come back tomorrow," he groaned. "We're closed."

"Oh, thank the Gods," she said. "I've got to get you inside. Can you get up?"

"Charlotte?" Julian's teeth were chattering. "That you?"

"It's me. Come on before we freeze."

Charlotte helped Julian up.

"Ow!" he yelled as he put weight on his right foot. He leaned onto Charlotte, nearly knocking her over.

"It might be broken," said Charlotte. "You'll need to let Keir take a look once we get off this mountain."

If they got off this mountain. Charlotte was much shorter and smaller than Julian and supporting him as they climbed the last steps of the snow-covered path to the dwarf's cottage was a challenge, especially on the stairs.

But when they made it to the door, it was clear no one was inside. "We have to go in," said Charlotte. "I hope he'll forgive us, but we'll die if we don't."

"Look," said Julian, kicking something on the ground with his good foot.

It was the curled-up corner of a sheet of paper. A note buried under the snow.

Charlotte picked it up and read it aloud.

Mr. Blair,

Hope you didn't come. I've left for the mines to ride out the storm. If you're here, stay as long as you need. I left some wood by the fire.

-   Thordin

Charlotte didn't need to be told twice. She pried open the door—it was tough against the cold wind with the weight of Julian on her shoulder, but she managed it. Inside, she gently helped him into the first chair she could find.

"I'll get the fire going," she said. When she turned back to look at him, he had removed his cloak and scarf and was taking off his shirt. She froze, panicking. "What are you doing?"

"My clothes are soaked. I fell coming up the path. I don't know how long I was there in the snow. Not long, I'm guessing, since I'm still alive. But I can't keep these on."

Fair enough. It wasn't like Charlotte minded nudity. Korrigan fashion could be a bit…minimalist, especially in the warmth of summer.

But it was different with Julian, at least it was now. She was sure they must have gone swimming in their underwear at least once as children, but things were different then.

"Aren't you freezing too? That hat of yours is soaked."

Julian's voice was right behind her, leaning on a dresser to hold himself up, but she was nervous to turn and see his state of undress.

"It's the korrigan magic," she explained. "I don't mind the cold and damp. Though the snow is a bit much. I'll feel fine once this fire is going."

It was beginning to catch now. The logs the dwarf had left were good and dry; they burned fast and clean.

"Hey," said Julian. He clearly wanted her to look at him.

Slowly, Charlotte turned, keeping her eyes up at the ceiling.

Out of her peripheral vision, she could see he'd kept his trousers on, although he'd removed his boots and socks. She relaxed a little, but then tensed again when she saw the way the firelight lit the muscles on his chest, casting shadows beneath them that must have been making them look more impressive than they really were.

Because they really did look impressive.

"What are you doing up here anyway? Come to take my business?" He smiled, and it was equal parts adorable and infuriating.

"I came looking for you. Gwenla found the note you left, and we realized you were in trouble."

"I thought that might have been the case. Well, you saved my life." He hobbled closer to her, keeping the weight off his right foot. "Thank you."

"We're not saved yet," she said, trying to ignore the blush climbing into her cheeks. "We still have to get off this mountain."

"Tomorrow," said Julian. "I'm sure it'll be over by then. If we wait until the afternoon, it may be melted."

"Are you mad? I can't stay here tonight. I have the wedding cakes to bake tomorrow."

"Are you mad? Have you seen it out there? The only way we're getting back down there right now is on our arses. You don't have a sled hidden under that hat, do you?"

Julian snatched the hat off Charlotte's head, releasing her silver hair.

"Hey!" she cried, reaching for it back.

But Julian had overestimated his ability to maneuver with one foot. He lost his balance trying to keep the hat away, careening towards the open fire. Charlotte caught him and pulled him to her, but the shock of grabbing his bare chest knocked her off her balance, sending them both to the floor by the hearth.

"Oof! Get off of me, you big oaf!" she said, trying to push her way out from underneath him.

"Are you sure you want that?" he asked. He untangled his bad leg from beneath her but otherwise stayed put.

Charlotte's head spun. She looked into his dark eyes. They were so dark and deep, she felt like she could drown in them.

"I don't—"

She stopped herself. She didn't know what she wanted to say. There was a part of her that didn't want to say anything at all. That wanted to pull him to her and give into the feelings that had been lurking in the back of her mind since the moment she saw him again.

But she couldn't. She pulled herself upright, and this time, he let her. "I'm still angry with you," she said.

"I know," said Julian. He sat across from her on the floor and crossed his legs as best as he could.

It brought her back to childhood again, back to the parlor of Weldan House, sitting together playing Five Stones on the floor, yelling and laughing until someone told them to be quiet.

"More than angry, I'm disappointed," said Charlotte, forcing herself to remember that this wasn't the same Julian. "I know what I did must have hurt you. I didn't expect you to forgive me right away or to forget what had happened. But I didn't expect you to hurt me back. I hoped that with time, we could be the friends that we were once again. Or maybe something more, if I'm being honest." If she was going to put it all out there, it might as well be all of it. "I don't think what we're asking for is unreasonable. I don't want you to fail. Maybe in a few years once all the things Prince Idris is building are done, Herot's Hollow will be big enough that we can have a dozen bakeries and plenty of business for all of them. But that's not where we are, and it's hurting us both to compete. Going it alone is hard, and I'm sorry that things have been so hard for you that you feel it's your only choice. But it isn't. You can be part of our community. We all need community sometimes. It's not always easy, and sometimes the compromises make you wonder if it's worth it. But then one day, you wake up and you find that you need help. Like I needed help from the korrigans. Like Mrs. Knox's sister needed help when she left."

Julian, who had been listening intently without interrupting, perked up at the mention of Mrs. Knox. "Mrs. Knox left?"

"She's coming back," said Charlotte defensively. "The bakery is staying open."

"But you're going to have to make the wedding cakes on your own. You need my help."

Charlotte scoffed. "No, I don't. I can manage—"

"You do. Admit it."

She did. She could manage, maybe, if she could get back in the morning. But any later than that, and she would need another pair of hands to keep to the schedule.

And maybe another oven.

"Fine," she said. "I was coming to see if I could use your new oven when the storm began. I could use your help. But mostly because I came up here to save you, and it might cost me a lot of time."

"Then you would've been better off if you hadn't helped me at all," said Julian.

"I wouldn't."

"Why not?"

Charlotte held herself perfectly still as she responded. "You know why not."

She watched the realization cross his face. *Because I care for you. Because I've always cared for you, no matter how much of an idiot you can be. Because if something had happened to you when I could've helped you, I would never have forgiven myself. Even if you never changed your mind. Even if I never forgave you. I still would have done it.*

"Charlotte," he said softly. Gods, it felt so good to hear him say her name, her true name, in spite of everything. "You're right," he said.

"What?" She was certain she hadn't heard him correctly. Did he just say she was right?

"You're right." He leaned towards her, his hand stroking a strand of her silver hair. "Charlotte, if you hadn't showed up when you had, I would have died out there. I realized it the moment I came to. I would have died because I twisted my ankle, and that's about the saddest way to go that I've ever heard. I've been such a godsdamn idiot. I charged up a mountainside in a blizzard for a handful of coin I don't even need. You were completely right, and I was wrong. I was going to say something, but you seemed to have such a lovely speech prepared—"

"You arsehole!" Charlotte took her wet scarf off and threw it at him.

Julian laughed, a deep belly laugh that reached his eyes. "It was good though, really. A little repetitive—"

Charlotte moved to get up. Julian caught her by the wrist.

"I'm sorry," he said, his laughter stopping. "I'm sorry. For everything. I want to help you. I want us to work together. I don't want to give up baking entirely—honestly, I love it. It brings me a lot of joy. But I'm sure we can work something out like you said. You supply the bread for my sandwiches; I give you cheese and the discount milk I get from my supplier in Sudport. Oh, and I'll need some of those chocolate biscuits. The worst part of this whole ridiculous feud I started has been missing out on those biscuits."

"That's the worst part?"

"No," admitted Julian. "Gods, I missed you, Charlotte. I didn't even realize how much until I saw you again. It all keeps flooding back in. So many memories. And then, you. The way you are now…" He looked Charlotte up and down, admiring without a hint of shame. "You're breathtaking."

Charlotte struggled to find the words to respond. "I—well—thank you."

Julian chuckled nervously. "I hope you don't mind me saying that. If you don't feel the same, that's alright. I'm happy to have you back in my life, whatever that looks like."

"No," said Charlotte. "I mean, I do. Feel the same about you." She sighed. "You're really good-looking. It's annoying, actually."

"Annoying?"

"Like it was hard to hate you when you looked like that." Julian leaned back, showing off his muscles, looking off into the distance with the smug superiority of someone who knew how good they looked. Charlotte rolled her eyes, but she quickly returned them to look at him. "In all honesty, I was surprised you were interested in me in that way."

Julian shifted back forward, leaning closer to Charlotte. "My interests are a little different. I'm only attracted to people I care about, and only seldomly even then. When I care about someone, it's about all of them. Not just what they call themselves or how they dress. Who they are."

Charlotte's heart raced in her chest. "Then you care about me?"

Julian pulled himself closer still, reaching for her face. "Yes, Charlotte. Of course I do. I always have."

He tilted her head back and kissed her, and this time, she kissed him back.

"There's only one bed in here," he said, looking around when he had come up for air. "But it would be madness to try to leave before the morning."

"We'll make do," said Charlotte.

⁂

They woke in the morning to find a couple feet of snow blocking them inside.

Charlotte tried to dig them out to no avail. Even if she could clear all the snow herself, how was she meant to carry Julian down the icy mountain with his broken foot?

"Come back to bed," murmured Julian. "The sun is out. We can wait for it to melt. I'll help you with the cakes when we get back. There's no hurry."

He had a point there, and the idea of spending a few hours with him under the blankets in the cozy cabin wasn't exactly unappealing.

Charlotte crawled back into bed. There was no need to hurry now that she had help.

They awoke again hours later to the sound of thunder.

No, not thunder. The thundering sound of foot-steps.

"The spriggan!" said Charlotte. "He can help us make it down the mountain."

"The what now?"

"It's a tree monster of sorts. It's friends with my brother. Well, it tried to kill him. But only the one time. Come on, get dressed."

Charlotte attempted to explain more as they dressed, but Julian remained fairly skeptical until they were outside.

"Mr. Spriggan! Mr. Spriggan, sir!" called Charlotte. Keir hadn't told her how to address it; she didn't want to be rude.

She couldn't see it, but she could see the shaking branches and the snow and ice falling from trees where he walked. He was very close.

"Ah, humans. Or something like them," he said when he approached, sensing Charlotte's magic. "What do you need from the forest?"

"We need your help getting down the mountain. We're making the cakes for Keir and Alison's wedding.

Or we're meant to, but Julian's hurt, and we need a lift. Can you help us?"

"Ah yes, the wedding. I'm going there too. Come along, little humans."

The spriggan was already taller than Charlotte had expected, but he grew even taller until reaching down to pick up Julian was nothing.

Julian yelled as the spriggan threw him over his shoulder. "Oh Gods! Please don't eat me!"

"This human is strange, sister of Keir," said the spriggan. "He thinks I am carnivorous."

"He's just frightened. Julian, it's okay! Are you okay?"

It took Julian a little time to respond, but he finally yelled down something that was sort of like a "yes."

"Would you like a lift too?"

"Yes, please," said Charlotte. She would have been fine walking in the melting snow, to be honest, but it just seemed like great fun to ride on the spriggan's shoulders down to the village.

And it was.

Chapter Nineteen

STAG NIGHT

Keir

Keir had just found out Charlotte had been missing when she returned.

The entire town had come out into the street to see the arrival of the spriggan, and Keir had almost missed her in his rush to get up the mountain after her.

"She's there, Keir, look!" Alison was pointing to the spriggan's shoulder, and sure enough, there was his sister, smiling and waving down at the crowd like royalty.

"And is that…Julian?"

Julian was clinging to the spriggan's neck, a branch wrapped around his waist, holding him upright.

"Here is good," said Charlotte from twenty feet in the air. "Julian needs to see my brother. Thanks for the ride!"

The spriggan gently lowered them both to the ground. Keir rushed to Charlotte first, but she directed him to Julian's ankle.

"I'm here for the wedding," said the spriggan as Keir examined Julian's range of movement and pain level.

"It's tomorrow," said Alison. "At the town hall."

"Very good," said the spriggan. "I'll plant right here." Keir had to look up from Julian's ankle to see what was going on. The spriggan stood in a patch of grass near the market square and extended roots down. Then he stood in place, looking for all intents and purposes like an ordinary tree. An ordinary tree with a face.

"What a town!" cried Alison's mother, hiccoughing.

"Mum, how many pints have you had?" said Alison, leading her mother back inside.

"The ankle isn't broken," said Keir. "But it'll take a bit of time to heal. You'd do best with a crutch. I have one at the house."

"But I'm needed on my feet. There are wedding cakes to make," said Julian.

Keir looked at Charlotte. What was she playing at this time? "What happened to Mrs. Knox?"

"She was called away on an urgent message from her sister. Julian has agreed to help me. Don't worry. We can do it."

The last time Keir had spoken to Charlotte about Julian, they were completely at odds, and she was furious about it. He must have missed something, but that wasn't a rare occurrence on its own.

"Isn't there something you can do?" asked Charlotte. "Some magic?"

Keir sighed. Alison wasn't nearby, and she'd never tried direct healing magic before anyway. Keir himself had, but it been the disaster that had resulted in the vine that nearly swallowed the town.

He knew what he would have said a year ago before he'd met Alison. *Absolutely not. It's far too dangerous, and it probably won't work anyway.*

But he'd felt the magic when Alison wielded it. He had even wielded it himself to save his own life at Winwold College. He didn't fully understand it, and maybe he never would, but he had felt its limits. Felt the will that had denied him before. Whatever force lay beneath it, it could be bargained with. Persuaded.

Idris had told him it was a negotiation, but Keir hadn't understood what he was offering in the bargain.

But as he looked at his sister, he knew what he needed to offer it.

It was a part of himself that he offered. A vulnerable, humble part of himself that understood that there were things in this world beyond explanation, and that if those things would take what they needed from him, he might be given something in return.

Keir turned to Julian's ankle. It was a simple sprain; one of the outer ligaments was likely pulled, maybe even torn very slightly. It would heal on its own within a few weeks.

Or it could heal right this moment. It wasn't complex. The ligament just needed to stitch itself back together, like pulling together threads to sew a wound shut. Keir visualize sewing it shut with an invisible needle.

"Is it working?" asked Charlotte.

"Shh," said Keir. "Let me concentrate."

He felt in his chest for the place the magic came from. It was harder to find without Alison nearby, but just the thought of her led him to it. He imagined pulling the magic from that place and threading it onto a needle.

When he pulled, the magic resisted slightly. He pulled back quickly, feeling the panic come over him. Was he doing the wrong thing again? Would this backfire and end up hurting them all?

He felt Alison approaching without even turning to see her, the magic in him sensing the magic in her.

"Keir's trying to heal Julian's ankle," explained Charlotte, seeing Alison's confusion. "With magic."

Alison was surprised. "Do you need my help?" she asked.

"Maybe," said Keir. "I know what needs to be done. But I'm not sure how to 'negotiate,' as Idris calls it."

"Open yourself to it," said Alison. "Let it feel your fear and doubt. Don't try to hide it. It's okay to be afraid. Let yourself feel it, and then move on to making it better."

Keir was afraid, but he trusted Alison more than anything in the world. He tried again, feeling for the magic within him. There it was, stronger now with Alison near him. He pulled on it again, just a thread. He felt the resistance and the fear it caused him. He sent the fear into the magic.

And then he sent in Alison's reassurance. The relief of her presence. The comfort of her touch.

The magic released for him. It was his magic, not Alison's, and though he felt her love and support through their bond, he felt that the power was his alone to control.

Slowly, carefully, he threaded an invisible needle in his mind. Even more slowly, he stitched the tear in Julian's ankle together. The magic had made it visible to him somehow, not as an image but as a feeling. He could feel when it was made whole.

"Gods, it doesn't hurt at all," said Julian. "Look, the swelling is gone. Unbelievable."

"Amazing," said Alison, kissing Keir on the cheek. "You're a healer."

"You're going to be the most popular doctor in Wilderise," said Charlotte. "Thanks for the help."

"Be careful on it for a few days," called Keir, but Julian was already practically running to his shop, with Charlotte close behind him. "I don't know if it will last."

"I don't think they care," said Alison.

"What was that about?" said Idris, coming out of the inn. "You were supposed to be getting ready for the party. The carriage is heading to Fossholm any minute now."

"I'm so proud of you," said Alison. "I'll see you tonight when you get back?"

"*If* I get back," said Keir.

Idris had an entire route planned out for Keir's stag night. They started at a distillery just outside of Fossholm. The elf who owned it was thrilled to share his pride and joy with the prince, a 250-year single malt whiskey.

"None of the fire, all of the warmth," said the elf.

"We need a bit of fire too," said Idris, although he didn't decline the ancient drink. "In fact, I prefer it."

"Of course, your highness. How about a trip through time? We can start with our youngest, the twelve-year. She's a feisty lass."

Keir worried about drinking so much the night before his wedding, but he knew if he mentioned it to Idris, the prince would make sure he drank even more. He took only a sip from each glass, tipping out the remainder into a potted plant when no one was looking.

Even from just a sip, Keir found he had a taste for the oldest, most expensive whiskies that they tried. But he was in luck: in honor of the patronage of Prince Idris and his upcoming nuptials, he was gifted a 100-year bottle that cost a ludicrous 500 gold ordinarily.

The next stop was the inn in Fossholm, the one they'd frequented in the summer when they were scheming to stop the construction of the dam. There, they shared several pitchers of beer and a dinner of roasted meats and hearty vegetables, all of it dripping with butter. It was by no means a healthy meal, but Keir was grateful to have something in his belly to soak up all the booze.

Then they went to a new establishment up the High Street: a public house that had recently opened in hopes of capitalizing on the king's investment in Wilderise. Its specialty was gins; Keir found them more dangerous than the whiskies as they were far easier to drink. At least the addition of tonic water made them marginally healthier, although they were unlikely to encounter malaria this far north.

By the time they boarded the carriages back to Wilderise to visit the inn there as the last stop, Keir was well and truly off his gourd despite his best efforts to moderate his drinking. He wasn't alone: Leo was singing Gallic songs entirely by himself that Yordin was dancing to; Duncan and Nigel were kissing, heavily; and Brytak and Idris were throwing coins out of the carriage for the "fairies," which were nowhere to be seen. Only Weyland seemed to have retained any sense, possibly due to his size advantage on the rest of them, but even he belched loudly a few times.

When they arrived at the inn in Herot's Hollow, Julian was just arriving.

"Wedding cakes down?" said Keir. He was impressed by how sober he sounded. Maybe he wasn't as bad off as he'd thought.

"Down?" asked Julian. "Oh, you meant 'done.' Yes, for the most part. The last bits of decorating will be done in the morning."

"Join us!" yelled Idris. He put his arm around Julian's neck. "This one is getting hitched," he said, grabbing Keir by the neck with his other arm.

Julian laughed. "I know. I've spent the last several hours making his cake with his sister."

"Oh, right," said Idris. "Well, you've earned a drink. Cheers!"

Keir had no idea what Idris thought he was toasting with: his hand was empty.

"Come on," said Keir. "Let's get inside before they throw us out of town."

"Who's gonna do that?" slurred Idris. "I'm—*hic*—the prince."

"Maybe him," said Leo, pointing to a squat dwarf running their way in a constable's uniform.

"Stop right there, Craig! I see you. You won't get away." The dwarf was chasing someone, or trying to, at least. He was barely moving faster than a walk. "Lord Wexenas! He's getting away."

Keir had heard that name before—the constables from Fossholm that had bothered Alison about the stolen ink. And he knew the other name as well—Mr. Craig, the thatcher who tried to get her to overpay for her roof repair, who was wanted for a similar crime.

"There," said Brytak. "He's across the river. Heading down Orchard Lane."

The dwarf constable was going to lose him, that was for sure. And then he'd be on Keir's property somewhere.

That just wouldn't do.

"Let's get him, boys!" yelled Keir, leading the group in a run across the river.

They caught up to the constable nearly immediately, overtaking him as he objected to their interference. "Stop! This is a matter for the law!"

"I *am* the law," yelled Idris. "Stop, thief! Your prince—*hic*—commands it!"

They ran past him, gaining on Mr. Craig, who realized he was trapped in a wall-lined lane with nowhere to go but over a gate.

He chose Alison's gate to jump—that was the wrong choice.

"You will not harm my bride," yelled Keir. "Get back here, you cur!"

Inside Alison's property, there weren't many good options. The orchards and fields were bare and offered no cover. His only choices were the woods beyond and the hedge maze, and he chose wrong again.

"He's in the maze!" yelled Keir.

Keir knew Alison's maze well by now. It only had a couple of turns, and even without seeing which way he'd went, he knew how to stop him.

"Idris!" Keir reached back for Idris's hand. He felt the surge of the prince's magic, which he directed at the hedges, forcing them to grow over and close the only other exit.

A young elf in a constable's uniform was right behind them. Lord Wexenas, Keir presumed.

"Stand back, we'll take it from here. Tirrin, I've got him," said the elf. "Gods, it's you, my Lord. My apologies," he said, spotting Keir. And then he saw the man beside Keir. "Oh. Your royal highness. Oh, heavens help me."

Lord Wexenas fainted.

They had just closed in on Mr. Craig when Tirrin, the dwarf constable, finally arrived.

"I've got him," said Tirrin. "Thanks for the assist, boys. I can take it from here."

"And what of this one?" asked Idris, tapping the unconscious Lord Wexenas with his shoe.

"He'll be fine," said Keir, bending to check.

"Would one of you mind hauling him back to the inn?" said Tirrin as he tied Mr. Craig's wrists. "I've got my hands full."

Weyland threw Lord Wexenas over his shoulder, and they followed him from the maze as Idris reopened the other exit.

"Someone's been practicing their magic," he said to Keir.

"I'm sorry for taking some of your power," Keir replied. They were old friends, but perhaps stealing each other's magic was a level of intimacy they didn't share yet. "I panicked."

"Don't be. I'm not sure I could've aimed it straight if you had asked. I probably would've grown a second hedge maze on top of the first one."

As they headed back towards the street, they found Alison's entire hen-night party standing outside the back of her cottage, come to see what all the commotion was about.

"We caught the thief!" yelled Idris.

"Hi, Alison. I love you," yelled Keir. All the running and the magic had him really feeling it now. "Idris, did you know that I love her?"

"Shut it, you. You'll put her off you," said Idris. "Have fun, girls!"

"We will," said Rinka.

"Have fun and be careful," called Alison after them.

She was such a gem. Just one more night, and they'd belong to each other forever.

Chapter Twenty

THE WEDDING

Alison

The girls had enjoyed a considerably quieter night than the boys, judging by their encounter in Alison's garden.

They had started the evening with a lovely ritual Lady Sibba had found in a book in the town archives. They went out to the standing stone circle at the border of Alison and Keir's properties and shared a bottle of sparkling wine in some fancy goblets Rinka had found at Weldan House.

"The goblets symbolize the feminine vessel," Lady Sibba read. "We share them and the bonds of sisterhood in this golden circle."

"Cheers!" said Rinka, holding up her glass.

"Not yet," said Lady Sibba. She continued reading. "We anoint the bride-to-be and give our blessing for her happy marriage."

"Anoint?" asked Alison. It was getting pretty cold out with the sun setting. She wasn't sure she wanted to be covered in wine.

"Oh, there's meant to be a cup of oil," said Lady Sibba. "You just dab a little on the forehead."

"I've got it," said Gwenla. "Won't be a minute." The old dwarf hurried off back to the cottage.

"Do you suppose the order of the ritual matters?" asked Ceri, shivering.

"I doubt it," said Lady Sibba. The elf clutched her heavy cloak to her chest. Even though she was dressed the most warmly, she also seemed the least comfortable.

"Let's keep going," said Alison. "We can come back to the anointing."

"Okay, where were we? Ah, yes. 'We shower her with flowers to symbolize fertility.'"

There weren't many flowers blooming at this time of year, but Gwenla had managed to scrounge up a few of the later camellias. It seemed a shame to tear their perfect little petals, but magic demanded sacrifices.

Gwenla made it back in time to shred her own camellia on Alison, and then she dabbed a drop of oil on

Alison's head. "Not too much. I don't want you to be greasy and have spots on your wedding day."

"Last thing," said Lady Sibba. "We raise our glasses to toast the bride's health and good fortune. Cheers!"

"Cheers!" they all said.

"Quick, let's get back inside," said Alison.

They followed her into the cottage, where they shared tea, biscuits, and the kind of story about their partners that would have made Alison's mother blush (thankfully, she'd turned in early at the inn).

Charlotte had just joined them for a final drink before they turned in themselves when they heard the chaos outside.

"That'll be Idris," said Rinka. "It always is when there's this much of a racket."

She was right, of course, but it wasn't just him. Just about every man in town came out of Alison's hedge maze. Alison was glad to see Mr. Craig apprehended— she was still sore about her treatment with the roof— and even more glad still to see Keir.

He looked like he was having a great night. His collar was undone, and his dark hair was a mess on his head, but his cheeks were flushed with joy. She knew this kind of rowdy partying wasn't really his preference, but she was glad he'd participated in the tradition. And apparently far from getting into trouble themselves, they'd actually stopped a trouble-maker who was on the loose.

"Those will be our husbands," Alison said to Rinka. She glanced at Ceri, who smiled, and she even dared to glance at Charlotte, who blushed. She'd read the Julian situation correctly, then.

"Let's get to bed," said Rinka. "We need our beauty sleep. Some of us have somewhere to be in the morning, although those boys don't seem to know it."

⸎⸏⸎

In the morning, Alison and Rinka got ready in Julian's bakery, which was one of the only places in town to have fully functioning 'lectrics. Julian and Charlotte finished their work on the wedding cakes (they refused to let Alison see them until they were finished) while Rinka curled Alison's hair with the 'lectric curler Keir had bought her.

Ceri came by and offered them some pointers she'd picked up from Ana, her roommate whose mother was a hair stylist back in Turtle Island. "Curl them tight so they'll stay. Then we'll brush them out to make them look more natural."

Ceri was nice enough to help them with their makeup, although Rinka was quite accomplished with it herself.

"I'm grateful to have you both," said Alison when she saw herself in the looking glass. There were neat lines around Alison's blue eyes that she never could have managed herself, and her lips were done in a soft plum lipstick that she'd borrowed from Ceri.

"You're so lovely," said Rinka, brimming with pride.

"You as well."

Everyone was looking their best, it turned out. Rinka had made Alison wait until Keir was already in the town hall so he wouldn't see her before the big moment, but Alison saw most of the town come by after him. It was such a delight to see everyone in their finest clothes.

"Who are they?" asked Ceri, pointing through Julian's shop window to a couple making their way up the High Street.

It took Alison a moment to recognize them. The fairies Genn and Mab had somehow taken Fulling height once more, even though they were no longer in the fairy world. "They're the rulers of the fairies, I think," said Alison. "Or at least the ones in Wilderise. I'm not sure how any of it works."

"They're spectacular," said Ceri. Genn was wearing a fine suit in a blue that perfectly matched the sky, while Mab wore a long gauzy dress in a pale lavender that seemed to shimmer as she walked. Both of them kept their folded wings behind them, but their white feathers seemed to float behind them like wisps of fog.

Alison laughed as a long-furred creature with floppy ears went running by next—Barney the dog was being chased by Yordin's children, all of them except for Finnli, who was walking calmly along with Willow. "I bet Willow is furious, but Barney seems to be having a good time."

"The cakes are done," said Charlotte, joining them in the front, "if you wanted to sneak a quick peek before you head over. We'll bring them around after the ceremony."

Alison went to the back (with Rinka holding her train), and she couldn't believe what she saw.

"They're a work of art," she said. She walked around each cake, admiring it from every angle (and forcing poor Rinka to work very hard not to tangle the lace of her train). The white cake had a cascade of sugar flowers in pink, yellow, and blue, with a few real pansies mixed in that were almost indistinguishable from the ones they made. The chocolate cake was glazed to a mirror shine with a simple "A" in the center that looked as though it had been embossed somehow.

"I can't believe you made them," said Alison. Then she realized how rude that sounded. "No offense, Charlotte. I know you're new to baking. When you said Mrs. Knox had to leave, I thought you'd make us something simple. I never expected this. They're incredible. Thank you. Thank you both."

"Of course," said Charlotte, giving Alison a hug. "Welcome to the family."

Just then, there was a knock at the door.

It was Mab, and in her hands were bouquets of flowers that were out of season: peonies, roses, sprays of lavender, and quite a few flowers Alison had never seen before. "Hello again, Alison Lennox. I went to the town hall, and the aisle was bare. No flowers to speak of. You can't have a wedding without flowers. I've gone to the liberty of adding a few. I hope you'll accept these bouquets as a token of our congratulations."

"Thank you, Mab. But how did you manage? There aren't many flowers in winter."

"Not in Wilderise, but there are warmer places. The fairy world has many doors."

Alison had a lot of questions about travel in the fairy world, but she would have to find out at another time. It was time to head to the town hall.

"Are you ready to be Mrs. Ainsley?" asked Rinka.

"Oh," said Alison, touching the locket on her chest that held her father's picture. In all the madness of planning, Alison had forgotten to decide what to do about her name. She still wasn't certain what she wanted, whether she could give up that link to her father forever. She decided to make the choice in the moment—she'd know what felt right then. "I'm ready to be Keir's wife, at least."

When they arrived at the town hall, they quickly realized that Mab had been operating under a different definition of "few" when she described the flowers she added.

"My Gods, it's beautiful!" said Rinka. Every inch of wall was covered in a magnificent display of floral color from all around the world. The aisles were adorned at the ends with elaborate arrangements, and a path of white petals led to a grand archway at the back with Weyland's anvil beneath it.

Underneath the arch stood Gwenla, and beside her, there was Keir.

Alison had seen Keir done up in his best suit before at the balls at Weldan House, but there was something different about him now. It was in his posture, she realized. She'd never seen him stand straight and tall in all the time she had known him; he'd always seem weighted, as if something sat on his shoulders that kept him from being upright.

Whatever that had been had lifted now. He was light as a feather. When his eyes met hers, his mouth fell open in awe.

Alison could feel his magic from across the room. He'd opened it to her, inviting her in.

She returned the gesture. As if of their own volition, the petals in the aisle lifted into the air and then drifted slowly back down like snowfall as Alison walked down it.

Alison only realized when she reached the end that Rinka must have followed her and that Idris was there standing next to Keir. She looked around at the guests: her family and Keir's in the front row, all of their friends behind them. It was all happening so fast, it overwhelmed her.

Keir took her hand, and she was back on solid ground again. "You're beautiful," he whispered to her.

"Dear friends and honored guests," began Gwenla. "We've come here today in the sight of the Gods to witness the bond of Dr. Keir Ainsley, Marquess of Caernock, and Miss Alison Lennox of Herot's Hollow in holy matrimony. Now, believe it or not, I'm no vicar."

There was laughter from the crowd.

"I'm here because I'm a friend to these two lovely humans, and they've asked me to join them together because that's apparently something that's allowed in this country. All I really have to do is pronounce them husband and wife and strike this anvil—" Gwenla patted the anvil with one hand, "—with this here hammer," she said, holding up a golden hammer

Weyland must have made for the occasion. "That's really all it takes."

Keir and Alison laughed at that. Maybe that's all they should have done. But Alison was excited to share her vows with Keir at least, and she knew Gwenla would give her a chance to do so.

"But before I do, I do want to say something about marriage. I met the love of my life later in my life than most, certainly later than these two have. And at times, I've regretted that I didn't have longer to share with her, but one thing I know about marriage: every moment I spent married to her was worth every moment of pain I've felt after losing her. If I could go back and do it over, I wouldn't change a thing, even the times that were hard. A marriage isn't a guarantee of a lifetime of happiness, but it's a promise that no matter what comes, you'll have someone to face it with. Even when you lose them that's true, because to marry someone is to carry them with you always."

Gwenla choked up a bit on the last words. Alison took her hand and squeezed it. "Thank you, love," Gwenla whispered.

"Alison, I believe you've prepared your own vows."

Alison had written them down, but she'd read them so many times that she didn't need to look. Instead, she looked into Keir's eyes as she spoke. "Keir," she began, and then she felt a little sob. "Sorry, sorry," she said to the crowd.

Keir reached into his breast pocket and handed her his handkerchief. She dabbed at her eyes, hoping she hadn't ruined the eyeliner. "Keir," she tried again. "When I met you, I was searching for something. I didn't know what it was, but I knew something had been missing in my life. I expected to find the answer in what I'd always known: numbers, coin, the tangible things that I valued. The things that had always made sense to me even as they failed to give my life the purpose and meaning that I didn't realize I needed.

"Meeting you, knowing you, learning who you were and what you'd been through, how you gave so much of yourself to those around you despite what it had cost you, it gave me a purpose. I wanted to help you, but not just for your sake, but for the sake of this incredible town, this community of people that has made me feel for the first time in my life that I belong.

"I am honored that you allowed me into your life. I am humbled that you all have let me into your community. I am grateful that through our love, I have connected with a part of myself I didn't know existed. I feel that connection now between us, and I know that with it, we can do anything.

"I vow to stand by your side, wherever life takes us. I vow to be your partner, to share in life's joys and worries together as equals. I vow to be your strength when you are weary, to be your comfort when you are troubled, and to be your light on your darkest days."

Alison felt Keir's love surge through his magic. "That was amazing," he whispered. "Thank you."

"Keir, I believe you have something prepared as well."

Alison's eyes widened in shock. "What?"

"Surprise," said Keir, and a few people in the crowd chuckled. "You didn't think I'd let you be the only one, did you?"

Alison's heart pounded. She'd expected Keir to recite the ordinary vows, and she had been fine with it—she knew he was nervous when speaking in public, and she didn't doubt how he felt.

But to hear him say how he felt in front of everyone? It was an unexpected gift.

"Alison," said Keir. "Alison, I—" He paused, turned to the side to collect himself. There were tears in his eyes when he looked back at her. "Alison. I'm not as gifted with words as you are, so I hope you'll bear with me as I do my best to explain what you mean to me."

Alison nodded in encouragement.

"I told you once that you saved my life. That the life I led before I met you was half a life, hardly worth living at all. What you may not realize is that you save my life every day.

"I wasn't blessed with good humor. I often find things difficult and upsetting that don't seem to bother other people. I carry the weight of every mistake with me, every poor choice and bad decision I've made. I carry them even if they turn out well in the end." He glanced at Charlotte as he said this. Alison knew that having Charlotte back had eased much of his guilt, but their years apart meant it would never be erased entirely.

"I tell you this not because I think it makes me a promising future husband, but because it's who I am. I have always felt less than enough.

"But when I'm with you, I can see the possibilities that elude me on my own. It's not that I no longer feel my burdens. It's that when you share in them, I can see them as opportunities rather than challenges. I've told you that you make me want to be better. But the truth is, you make me better, every day I spend with you, just by being who you are.

"I've spent a lot of time wondering what it is that I can offer you. How is it fair that I take so much from you and offer you so little? But maybe that's my melancholy speaking again. Maybe I am blind to the good that I do, but I can see its impact on you. I can see that you're happy, and I can believe that I am some small part of it. And I'd never do anything to take that away from you.

"And so that is what I promise you. I vow to honor you, to respect you, to support you in every one of life's adventures, no matter what the little voice in my head says. I vow to trust you more than I trust myself because I know you have my best interest at heart. I vow to appreciate the joy and beauty you bring into my life and to welcome light and laughter into our home, in whatever form that may take. I vow to love you for the rest of my days and for whatever may come after. I love you, Alison."

Alison was fully crying now, the handkerchief streaked with the black of her makeup, and she didn't even care.

"I love you too," she said. "That was wonderful."

"Do we have the rings? And the ribbon?" asked Gwenla.

Finnli came forward with a ring box, and Idris produced a white ribbon from his pocket.

Alison hadn't yet seen the ring Weyland had made for her. He'd made it to match the engraving on her engagement ring, and it was really lovely.

"Thanks, Weyland," she said to him. He was down in the second row.

"You're welcome," he said, and the crowd laughed.

"With these rings, you share your oaths."

Keir placed the ring on Alison's finger, his hands shaking a bit from the nerves of it all. It fit like a glove.

Then Alison gave Keir his ring. She imagined holding his hands, years later when they had wrinkled, and seeing the ring still in the same place.

Gwenla tied the white ribbon over their hands. "With this ribbon, you bind your spirits together for all time."

She paused for a moment for effect, then she raised the hammer above the anvil. "By the power vested in me by this crazy place that apparently lets anyone do this, I now pronounce you husband and wife." She struck the anvil with a loud *plink!*

Keir leaned forward, kissing Alison as the crowd clapped.

He was her husband. She was his wife.

"Now let's have some cake!" yelled Gwenla, and everyone cheered.

Keir was as impressed by the cakes as Alison had been, and he was very interested to hear Alison's news that she thought Julian and Charlotte might be together now.

"We'll have to see when we're dancing," he said in between mouthfuls of chocolate frosting.

They signed the marriage certificate after the cake. It was time to make a choice, and Alison had been right—what she wanted to do was clear now with Keir beside her as her husband. "I'd like to be Alison

Lennox-Ainsley, if that would be alright with you," she told him.

"Of course," he said, opening the locket to see the pictures of Alison's father and his mother. "I'd like that as well."

"Dr. Keir Lennox-Ainsley, Marquess of Caernock? It's a bit of a mouthful," said Alison.

"No more than Mrs. Alison Lennox-Ainsley, Marchioness of Caernock."

"Touché."

"You do know Gallic after all," said Keir, laughing and kissing her on the forehead as he signed the certificate.

There were a number of toasts; Idris's came as something of a shock to the people who didn't know him well enough to know what he was like, and Rinka's was equally as funny as it was sweet. Alison demanded an end to it after her mother's toast: she was starving.

They enjoyed a meal Gwenla had cooked with Mr. Rainey in the inn's kitchen: roast beef from Brytak's family's farm and lamb from Aras's flock, cheese from Julian shop, and vegetables from Gwenla's root cellar. Julian brought several bottles of wine for them to share, and Idris had gotten a crate of the fiery whiskey they enjoyed the night before delivered.

By the time Nigel Smalls began to play his mandolin, with Duncan Corbett accompanying him on the town hall's pianoforte, they were all quite warm and full.

"Come, my darling. I wish to dance with my wife," said Keir, leading her to the dance floor.

Alison regretted that she hadn't practiced when Keir pulled her in. He was such an incredible dancer.

"Perhaps you can teach me," said Alison. "If you're looking for something you can do for me."

"With pleasure," said Keir.

They danced the night away, couples old and new, friends taking turns with friends. Brytak did get his dance from Eloise—Keir had brought five gold for Rinka, knowing he was likely to be wrong. Charlotte and Julian were inseparable; Idris and Rinka were entirely too much as usual, dramatically tangoing to a simple folksy tune; Weyland and Lady Sibba were sweet together, gently swaying to the music; Alison's mother enjoyed a few lively dances with Tomasar and Genn, who found her enchanting; Ceri was swept off her feet by the surprisingly elegant Leo, who was much less clumsy on the dance floor than off it; and even the spriggan joined in for a time, his branches creaking from the movement. Alison was sad when it was over, but she was also exhausted and ready for bed.

As they made the turn onto Orchard Lane, Keir turned to Alison. "Which house: yours or mine?"

"They're both ours now," she said. "Either way is fine."

They settled on Alison's cottage—it was closer—but whether her tiny cottage, Keir's larger stone house, or even the absurd mansion that was Weldan House someday, it didn't matter. Home was here, wherever Keir was. Wherever her friends were.

Wilderise was her home.

Epilogue

A few months later, Alison had Gwenla, Charlotte, and Julian to the cottage for tea while Keir was at Mrs. Knox's checking on her sister's hip, which had healed even better than expected thanks to a bit of quiet magic.

The Knox sisters were planning the trip of a lifetime to the continent and beyond, which would leave Charlotte in charge of the bakery for the longest period since Lupercalia. But Charlotte's baking had come a long way since then, Alison observed, as she sampled a delicate Gallic dessert that seemed to be made of a thousand layers of pastry filled with a light custard and topped with an intricate swirl of chocolate and cream icing.

"How in the world did you make this?" asked Alison. It looked like witchcraft to someone who could barely fry an egg.

"The icing is easier than it looks," said Charlotte. "You just sort of glob it on and run it through with a toothpick."

"The pastry isn't easy, though," said Julian.

"I used the docking technique you showed me," said Charlotte, smiling brightly at him. And then, turning to Alison and Gwenla, "It's a method of pricking the dough with a fork to keep it nice and flat when it bakes. My first go was a bit lumpy."

"Still delicious, though," said Julian.

Alison was glad to see the two of them getting along so well. On more than one occasion, she went into town to find they'd switched shops, with Charlotte helping to sell the wine while Julian enjoyed some time exchanging baking techniques with Mrs. Knox.

And she was glad to see that Charlotte had found a way to settle back into the life she had abandoned. It was good to have her home, for everyone's sake.

The door into the cottage opened, letting in the fragrant smell of the gardenia growing just outside.

"Don't get up," said Keir, dropping his bag on the desk. Gwenla was already halfway to the kitchen to pour him some tea. "I've got the post here."

He had quite a stack in his hands. He tilted the stack back to reveal a small package at the bottom. "This one is from Northern Publishing."

"Open it!" said Gwenla from the kitchen.

"I'll open that one last," said Alison. She was a bit nervous about what was inside.

On the top was a postcard with a lovely illustration of a cove with gentle waves washing up onto a sandy shore. "It's from Weyland," said Alison.

"Is that one of his?" asked Charlotte. "I had no idea beaches could look like that."

It was indeed one of Weyland's drawings, Alison saw from the signature at the bottom. She pointed it out to Charlotte.

"Are they still at the Rock?" asked Gwenla, returning with Keir's tea. "Are they ever coming back?"

"Let's see," said Alison.

Alison and Keir,

Hope all is well at home. Two surprises for you:

1) *We're finally heading back. As reassuring as your update was regarding Duncan's turn as a substitute, Sib can't make it one more day away from the school.*

2) I finally did what we discussed at Winter Solstice. And it turns out, Sib couldn't make it one more day without being my wife either, so we'll be returning to you as a married couple. The picture on the front is where it happened. Not bad for a village blacksmith, eh?

Let me know when you hear about the book.

All our love,
Weyland and Sibba

"Married!" said Gwenla. "You knew about this?"

"He asked me to help pick out the ring, but I didn't think they'd get married straight away," said Alison.

"How romantic," said Willow. The cat had just come through the flap in the back door.

Alison raised her eyebrows at Willow, who was usually a relentlessly practical creature.

"Well, it is," she said. "And a lot less of a fuss than your wedding."

"I didn't think you minded the fuss at our wedding," said Keir. "Without the fuss, there would have been no guests. And no guests would have meant—"

"No Barney," said Willow. "Alright, it was worth it for that. But Gwenla, if I never see any of those nieces and nephews of yours other than Finnli again, it will be too soon."

"You and me both," said Gwenla with a laugh. Willow hopped into her lap, and Gwenla set down her tea to give her a cuddle.

"This one is from Ceri," said Alison, holding up an envelope of fine stationary.

My dear friend Alison,

I'm sending along the list you requested of courtiers that I believe may be willing to support your land preservation initiative. I hope it's helpful.

Alison, a new member of the king's court now that she had married a marquess, had decided to return to their idea of permanently preserving parts of the Hill Country as a Place of Outstanding Natural Beauty. It might mean some time at court to convince others to support their cause, but it would be worth it to preserve the character and natural charm of Herot's Hollow for generations to come.

The letter continued:

We're doing well, thank you for asking. We've come home to the castle for the Beltane holidays. Leo is having the best time measuring all the ancient objects here. Father doesn't quite know what to make of him, but he's got his hands full with the trip to Wilderise anyway. (I'm not sure if Rinka told you, but we'll all be arriving at the end of the term. Lord Ainsley included, unfortunately.) Then Leo and I are on to Gallia to meet his (rather large) family before the beginning of fall term.

Let's get tea when we get to town. I need to catch you up on the court gossip before your debut as the marchioness.

With much love,
Ceri xx

"We'll figure it out," said Keir, squeezing Charlotte's hand at the news of the return of their father. "We could always take a holiday of our own somewhere. Maybe to the Rock to see that beach."

"No," said Charlotte. "I can't hide forever. I don't want to. He may not like it, but he has a daughter. Even if he never comes around, I won't keep pretending I don't exist."

"We'll stand by you, girl," said Gwenla. "Let him wail and moan if he must. You know who your real family is."

"Thank you," said Charlotte. "I do."

"What's in that one?" asked Keir.

Alison could guess what the large envelope was: it looked just like the one Rinka had sent her in the winter.

"The royal wedding announcement, I bet."

She was right.

The Wedding of the Century: Prince Idris to wed Rinka in picturesque Wilderise next spring!

The article was long and mostly pure speculation about who would be attending, which events would be happening and when, and what the future princess would be wearing, with a series of sketches from some of Loegria's most exclusive designers.

"I hope Lydiach is ready for all of this," said Alison, knowing who the real designer of Rinka's wedding dress would be.

"I hope we're all ready," said Gwenla. "There was a reporter here last week asking to see where the future princess stays when she's in town."

"You didn't tell them, did you?" asked Keir.

"Of course not," said Gwenla with a huff.

"They'll be more where they came from," said Julian. "Someone I barely knew in the city wrote me asking to stay next year. It's going to be madness."

Along with the magazine was a letter from Rinka:

My dearest Alison,

I've just arrived in the castle for the first time, and I so wish you were here with me. I can't believe this will all belong to me someday. I can't even decide if I want it to. If there was some way to have Idris without all of this, I'd take it in a heartbeat. I know he would too.

But it's not all bad. There's an incredible history to all of it. Much of it untold, I'm realizing. All we learn about in the history books is what these nobles were up to. Who was fighting whom, who married whom, which family owned which land. But there's an entire untold story here about the people who made it all possible. People who grew up like you and me, the people who built and cared for these great homes and families with their own sweat, blood, and tears.

Idris says there's a lot to learn from their stories, for his research into curses but also from a purely historical lens. I've decided to make it my mission to bring those stories to light, through the work of the new college and in my official role as princess, once that happens.

I can't wait to see you all again at the summer. Give our love to Keir and all the rest.

Love always,
Rinka

"That's a nice idea," said Gwenla. "She's always been such a champion of the working folk. I'm glad it'll be her in that castle one day."

"I'm glad it's not just Idris on his own. Can you imagine?" said Keir.

"I thought he was rather impressive," said Charlotte. "Until he came screaming out of the hedge maze, drunk off his arse."

They all laughed remembering the stag night the future king of Loegria and Wilderise had thrown.

"Are you going to open the last one?" asked Keir.

Alison picked up the last item in the pile: the package. It was wrapped in brown paper, but she could tell what it was before she even opened it.

It was her poetry book, bound in a lovely green cloth with gold foil on the cover.

Wilderise through the Seasons:
A Book of Poems by Alison Lennox-Ainsley,
Marchioness of Caernock
Illustrations by Weyland Gilroy

"Oh, let me see!" said Gwenla. "It's so lovely. Look at the color!"

Inside, Weyland's illustrations had been printed in full color with Alison's poems set inside them.

Alison flipped through the pages. She knew what each one held, but it was still surreal to see them bound up together in a proper book. It felt foreign, as if she'd picked it up in the bookstore in Sudport, not as if she'd made it herself with her own mind.

"There's a letter, too," said Keir, holding it out to Alison to read.

Dear Mrs. Lennox-Ainsley,

Thank you for sending your manuscript as requested. We've taken the liberty of printing a proof copy for your review. Please ensure that all pages have printed according to your desire.

We'd like to begin with a run of 1000 copies, to be distributed to stores here in Wilderise and in Loegria.

"One thousand copies!" said Gwenla. "Oh, what wonderful news!"

Enclosed you will find a contract for your review. We hope to hear from you soon, and congratulations on a job well done. (Our editor particularly enjoyed your poems regarding the spriggan. What an incredible imagination you have!)

Best,

Mr. Hamish McCrary, Northern Publishing

"Well done, my darling," said Keir. He gave Alison a quick kiss. "Is it what you want?"

Alison took the book back from Gwenla and looked at it. It was frightening, imagining the book in stores. Sitting on a shelf, being picked up by a stranger. The words she had put together, the stories from her real experiences (and some from her imagination, too, although obviously not the parts about the spriggan) being shared with the world. Was she ready for it?

She looked around at the faces of her friends and family, the beautiful home they'd built together, and the stack of kind regards from even those who were absent, and she knew what she wanted to do.

"I think I'm ready," she said.

"Wonderful!" said Gwenla. "Would you read it to us first?"

Alison was nervous to read her own words out loud, but here in Wilderise, anything was possible. "With pleasure," she said, and she opened the book to the first page and began to read.

THE END

Recipes

(Optionally) Spicy Brownies

Don't cheap out on the chocolate (including the cocoa powder); it makes a big difference. (If you're feeling lazy, just add ¼ tsp cayenne pepper to any old box mix before you add the wet ingredients. Be sure to mix well if you don't want to play spicy brownie roulette.)

1 cup (two sticks, 225g) unsalted butter
2 large eggs
1 cup (200g) sugar (granulated / caster)
1 tsp vanilla extract
½ cup (75g) all-purpose flour
¾ cup (75g) unsweetened cocoa powder
¼ tsp cayenne pepper (optional, to taste)
1 tsp salt
1 cup (125g) semisweet chocolate chips or buttons

1. Preheat the oven to 350°F (180°C/160°C Fan/Gas 4). Grease a 8 x 8 inch (20 x 20 cm) baking pan or line with nonstick baking paper.
2. Melt the butter in the microwave or a small saucepan over low heat until mostly liquid. Set aside to cool.
3. In a medium bowl, sift together or combine the flour, sugar, cocoa powder, cayenne pepper, and salt.
4. In a large bowl, beat together the eggs, sugar, and vanilla extract. Slowly add the flour mixture and the butter, making sure the butter has cooled to room temperature.
5. For very fudgy brownies (the best kind), stir for an extra minute or two past the point where the mixture is well-combined. Fold in chocolate chips.
6. Spread the batter in the pan with a silicone spatula. Bake for 40 to 45 minutes. A toothpick inserted in the center should come out mostly clean. (A few crumbs are okay.)
7. Cool for as long as you can wait. The very hot brownies will be difficult to cut, but they'll also smell (and taste) very good, and no one will judge you if you cut them a bit early.

Scones

The trick to good scones is to avoid overworking the dough. The technique is so similar to traditional buttermilk biscuits enjoyed in the Southern U.S. that I'm including my Papa's recipe and method for those as well, even though they aren't mentioned in the book. Serve the scones with jam (strawberry is most common) and clotted cream or butter. The biscuits are great with butter, apple butter, jam, or sausage gravy.

2 cups (250g) self-rising flour, plus extra for dusting surface
1 tsp baking powder
2 tbsp (25g) sugar
4 tbsp (½ stick, 55g) salted butter, chopped
1 large egg (plus 1 to brush tops, optional)
½ cup (120ml) whole milk

Optional fillings (use ½ cup / 100g or so):
Raisins or sultanas
Dried or fresh fruit (strawberries, blueberries, cranberries, or currants)
Cheese (grated, sharp cheddar works well. Omit the sugar if using.)

1. Preheat the oven to 425°F (220°C/200°C Fan/Gas 7). Grease a baking pan or cast-iron skillet.

2. Chop the butter cold from the fridge. Set aside to come to room temperature or soften for just a few seconds in the microwave.

3. In a large bowl, sift together or combine the flour, baking powder, and sugar (if using; omit for cheese scones). With a fork or pastry cutter, cut in the butter. Finish working the butter in with your fingertips, working quickly to prevent it from melting completely.

4. Create a well in the center of the bowl. Using the fork, stir the egg into the flour mixture. Slowly add the milk until the dough is sticky but workable. (You might not use all of it.)

5. Gently fold in fillings, if desired. Turn out the dough onto a lightly floured surface and press or roll with a rolling pin until 1 inch (3 cm) thick.

6. Cut with a lightly floured 2-inch (5 cm) round cutter or a sharp knife into triangles. Do not twist—it'll keep them from rising. Place into prepared baking tray or skillet. Leftover dough can be re-combined and cut again, but the second set of scones may not rise as well.

7. Brush the tops of the scones with leftover milk or another egg. Do not allow to drip down the sides.

8. Bake for 12-15 minutes until golden brown.

Old-fashioned Southern Buttermilk Biscuits

2 cups (250g) self-rising flour, plus extra for dusting hands
¼ cup (55g) vegetable shortening
1 cup (240ml) buttermilk
A bit of butter for brushing

1. Preheat the oven to 500°F (260°C/240°C Fan/Gas 8). Grease a round cake pan or cast-iron skillet.
2. Add the flour to a large bowl. With a fork or pastry cutter, cut in the shortening. Finish working the shortening in with your fingertips, working quickly to prevent it from melting completely.
3. Create a well in the center of the bowl. Slowly add the buttermilk until the dough is sticky but workable. (You might not use all of it, but this dough will be a bit stickier than the scone mixture.)
4. You can roll and cut them in the same way as the scones, but the traditional method is to make drop biscuits by shaping the dough into balls with floured hands. The biscuits should be large, "cathead" sized. Be careful not to incorporate so much flour that they become dry.
5. Place into prepared cake pan or skillet with sides nearly or barely touching and press lightly on top to flatten just a little bit. Don't be afraid to make a

"big biscuit" in the center of the pan if you have a lot of dough leftover; it's a treat to get the big biscuit.

6. Bake for 12-14 minutes until just browning on the top. Broil for an additional 1-2 minutes until tops are golden brown. Coat with butter while still in the pan.

Wedding Cookies (Biscuits)

I dare you to eat just one of these. They're so buttery and addictive. You can toast the nuts first if you're feeling ambitious to improve the flavor.

1 cup (2 sticks, 225g) unsalted butter
½ cup (60g) powdered (icing) sugar, plus ½ cup (60g) for rolling
½ tsp salt
1 cup (120g) almonds or pecans
3 tsp vanilla extract
2 cups (250g) all-purpose flour

1. Preheat the oven to 325°F (165°C/145°C Fan/Gas 3). Grease a cookie sheet or line with nonstick baking paper.

2. Set out the unsalted butter until it reaches room temperature. In a food processor or with a mortar and pestle, grind nuts until finely powdered.
3. With an electric mixer in a large bowl or a stand mixer, beat together butter, ½ cup powdered sugar, and salt until fluffy.
4. Gradually mix in vanilla, flour, and ground nuts until well-combined.
5. Roll into small balls (about 1 tbsp each) and arrange 1 inch apart on the prepared cookie sheet.
6. Bake 15 to 20 minutes until just golden.
7. Cool 10 to 15 minutes until safe to handle but still warm. Roll in remaining powdered sugar.

About the Author

Amy Yorke is an author of light and cozy fantasy and lover of all things magical and romantic. She is half English, half American, and she offers her sincere apology to readers of both languages for her idiosyncrasies in word choice. In her spare time, she enjoys gardening, playing video and tabletop games, and chasing after her cats.

Join her mailing list to receive news, updates, and promotions, including free advanced reader copies prior to new releases: https://www.amyyorke.com.